THE RIVAL RIGELIANS

MACK REYNOLDS

Table of Contents

THE RIVAL RIGELIANS

Mack Reynolds

COPYRIGHT INFORMATION

FOREWORD

HARDLY HAD MAN solved his basic problems on the planet of his origin than he began to fumble into space. Barely a century had elapsed in the exploration of the Solar System than he began to grope for the stars.

And suddenly, with an all but religious zeal, mankind conceived its fantasy dream of populating the galaxy. Never in the history of the race had fervor reached such a peak and held so long. The question of why was ignored. Millions of Earth-type planets beckoned and with a lemming-like desperation humanity erupted into them.

But the obstacles were frightening in their magnitude. The planets and satellites of Sol had proven comparatively tractable and those that were suited to man-life were quickly brought under his dominion. But there, of course, he had the advantage of proximity. The time involved in running back and forth to the home planet was meaningless and all Earth's resources could be thrown into each problem's solving.

But a planet a year removed in transportation or even communication? Ay! this was another thing and more than once a million colonists were lost before the Earthling could adapt to new climates, new flora and fauna, new bacteria—or to factors which the most far-out visionary had never fancied, perhaps the lack of something never before missed.

So, mad with the lust to seed the universe with their kind, men sought new methods. To a hundred thousand worlds they sent smaller colonies, as few as a hundred pioneers apiece, and there marooned them, to adapt, if adapt they could.

For a millennium each colony was left to its own resources, to conquer the environment or to perish in the effort.

A thousand years was sufficient. Invariably it was found, on those planets where human life survived at all, man slipped back during his first two or three centuries into a state of barbarism. Then slowly he began to inch forward again. There were exceptions and the progress on one planet never exactly duplicated that on another, however the average was surprisingly close to both nadir and zenith, in terms of evolution of society.

In a thousand years it was deemed by the Office of Galactic Colonization such pioneers had largely adjusted to the new environment and were ready for civilization, industrialization and eventual assimilation into the rapidly evolving Galactic Commonwealth.

Of course, even from the beginning, new and unforeseen problems manifested themselves....

—from *Man In Antiquity*
Published in Terra City, Sol
Galactic Year 3,502

CHAPTER I

THE CO-ORDINATOR looked out over the eighteen seated before him and said, "I suppose I'm an incurable romantic. You see, I hate to see you go."

Academician Amschel Mayer and Dr. Leonid Plekhanov sat slightly before the other sixteen. They were both in their early middle years and offset one another. Mayer was thin and high pitched, nervous and impatient; his manner was often that of a harried grade school teacher who disliked children. His colleague was heavy, slow and dour and he looked more the sergeant of infantry than a top political scientist.

Now, both showed their puzzlement, as did the balance of the team behind them.

The Co-ordinator added softly, "Without me."

Plekhanov kept his massive face blank. It wasn't for him to be impatient with his superior. Nevertheless, the ship was waiting, all stocked and ready for burn off. He stirred his bulk in his chair.

Amschel Mayer said, "It would be a pleasure if you could accompany us, Citizen." Inwardly, he realized the other man's position. Here was a dream coming true and Mayer and his fellows were the last thread that held the Co-ordinator's control over the dream. When they left, half a century would pass before he could again check developments.

The Co-ordinator took a deep breath and became more businesslike. "Very briefly, I wish to go over your assignment. Undoubtedly redundant, but if there are any questions, no matter how trivial, this is the last opportunity to air them."

What possible questions could there be at this late date? Plekhanov thought. He shifted his bulk again.

Behind him, Technician Jerome Kennedy whispered to the girl next to him from the side of his mouth, "Zen, I thought he was having us in for a last minute blast. A few snorts of guzzle."

Natalie Wieliczka said, "Shhhh."

The department head was swiveling slowly back and forth in his desk chair as he talked. "You are the first of many, many such teams. The manner in which you handle your task will affect man's eternity. Obviously, since upon your experience we will base our future policies on interstellar colonization." His voice lost volume. "The position in which you find yourself should be humbling."

"It is," Amschel Mayer agreed. Plekhanov nodded his head. Someone behind murmured further assent.

The Co-ordinator nodded too. "However, the situation is as near ideal as we could hope. Rigel's planets are all but unbelievably Earthlike. Almost all our flora and fauna have been adaptable. Certainly our race has been.

"These two are the first of the seeded planets. Almost a thousand years ago we deposited small bodies of colonists upon each of them. Since then, we have periodically checked from a distance, but never intruded."

His eyes swept the whole group, resting finally on the leaders. "No comment or questions thus far?"

Mayer said, when no one else could find a question, "This is one matter that has always surprised me. The colonies are so small to begin with. How could they possibly populate a whole world in one millennium?"

The Co-ordinator nodded and said, "Man adapts, Amschel. Have you studied the development of the United States in early history? During her first century and a half the need was for population to fill the vast lands wrested from the Amer-Inds. Families of eight, ten and twelve children were the common thing, and much larger ones were not unknown. And the generations crowded one against another. A girl worried about spinsterhood if she reached seventeen unwed. But in the next century? The frontier vanished, the driving need for population was gone. Not only were drastic immigration laws passed, but the family rapidly shrunk until by mid-Twentieth Century the usual consisted of two or three children, and even the childless family became increasingly common."

Mayer frowned impatiently. "But still, a thousand years. There is always famine, war, disease...."

Plekhanov snorted patronizingly. "Forty to fifty generations, Amschel? Starting with a hundred colonists? Where are your mathematics?"

The Co-ordinator said, "The proof is there. We estimate that each of Rigel's planets now supports a population of nearly one billion."

"To be more exact"—Natt Roberts spoke up from the rear of the group —"some nine hundred million on Genoa, seven and a half on Texcoco." His voice was as trim and neat as his physical appearance. However, it was information everyone present already possessed.

Mayer smiled wryly, "I wonder what the residents of each of these planets call their worlds. Hardly the same names we have arbitrarily bestowed."

"Probably, each call theirs *The World*," the Co-ordinator smiled. "After all, the basic language, in spite of a thousand years, is still undoubtedly

Amer-English. However, I assume you are familiar with our method of naming. The most advanced culture on Rigel's first planet is to be compared to the Italian cities during Europe's feudalistic years. We have named that planet Genoa. The most advanced of the second planet is comparable to the Aztecs at the time of the Spanish conquest. We considered Tenochtitlan, but it seemed a tongue twister, so Texcoco, the sister city of the Aztecs, is the alternative."

"Modernizing Genoa," Mayer mused, "should be considerably easier than the task of semi-primitive Texcoco."

Plekhanov shrugged heavy shoulders, in a manner betraying his Slavic background. "Not necessarily," he rumbled.

The Co-ordinator held up a hand and smiled at them. "Please, no discussion on methods at this point. An hour from now you will be in space with a year of travel before you. During that time, you'll have opportunity for discussion, debate and hair pulling on every phase of your problem."

His expression went more serious. "You are acquainted with the unique position you assume. These colonists are in your control to the extent that no small group has ever dominated millions of others before. No Caesar ever exerted the power that will be in your collective hands. For half a century, you will be as gods and goddesses. Your science, your productive know-how, your medicine—if it comes to that—your weapons, are many centuries ahead of theirs. As I said before, your position should be humbling."

Mayer said suddenly, unhappily, "Why not check upon us, say, once every decade? In all, our ship's company numbers but eighteen persons. Almost anything could happen. If you were to send a departmental craft each ten years..."

Kennedy whispered to Natalie Wieliczka, "Old Amschel's trying to hedge our bets."

She ignored him, making a prim moue.

The Co-ordinator was shaking his head. "Your qualifications are as high as anyone available. Once on the scene you will begin accumulating information which we here, in Terra City, do not have. Were we to send another group in ten years to check upon you, all they could do would be interfere in a situation with which they would not be cognizant."

Amschel Mayer shifted nervously. "But no matter how highly trained, nor how earnest our efforts, we still may fail." His voice worried. "The department cannot expect guaranteed success. After all, we are the first."

"Admittedly. Your group is first to approach the hundreds of thousands of planets we have seeded with our race. If you fail, we will use your failure to perfect the eventual system we must devise for future teams. Even your failure would be of infinite use to us." He lifted and dropped a shoulder in a wry gesture. "I have no desire to undermine your belief in your-selves but—how are we to know? Perhaps there will be a score of failures before we find the ideal method of quickly bringing these primitive colonies into our Galactic Commonwealth."

He came to his feet and sighed. He still hated to see them go. He said, "If there is no other discussion..."

He went from one to the other, shaking hands.

CHAPTER II

SPECIALIST JOSEPH CHESSMAN stood solidly before a viewing screen. Theoretically, he was on watch. Actually, his eyes were unseeing, there was nothing to see. The star pattern changed so slowly as to be all but permanent.

Not that every other task on board the spaceship *Pedagogue* was not similar. One man could have taken the craft from the Solar System to Rigel just as easily as the eighteen handcrew was doing. Automation at its ultimate, not even the steward department had tasks adequate to fill the hours.

He had got beyond the point of yawning, his mind was blank during these hours of duty. Inwardly, he was of the opinion that Mayer was an idiot to insist that the crewman standing bridge watch not be allowed to read. The scrawny old duffer never stood a watch himself, in spite of the fact that he was the nearest thing to a captain that the *Pedagogue* had.

Joe Chessman was a stolid bear of a man, short and massive of build. His face, even in repose carried a frown. He was the type who could step out of a barber chair and three minutes later have rumpled hair—the type who could purchase an expensive suit and in half an hour look as though he had slept in it.

A voice behind him said, low, throaty, "Hi, Spaceman. Need company?"

He turned and scowled at her.

"Those off watch aren't supposed to be on the bridge." He took in her outfit. "You look like you're going to a party." He paused and added. "Quite a party."

Isobel Sanchez smiled slowly. "I got tired of the everlasting coveralls. Don't you think this is an improvement?" She turned, for his inspection.

The inspection was rewarding. Isobel Sanchez had the lushness of her Iberian heritage. Her hair black, her complexion olive, her teeth unbelievably white behind equally unbelievably red, full lips. Considering her educational background, she was a remarkably beautiful woman, though in her face there was something not quite there. A something once called breeding.

Chessman growled sourly. "You better get back into your coveralls, Doctor Sanchez. Showing off that body of yours isn't going to help that ruling of Mayer and Plekhanov about the relations between members of the crew while we're in space."

He turned and stared at some of the control dials.

She came up beside him and pretended to look at them as well. And he became conscious of the breast pressing against his arm.

"What ruling?" she said innocently.

"No sex."

She drew back a step. "Well, really," she said. "Just because I've put on a dress for a change doesn't mean I'm trying to crawl in bed with you Citizen Chessman."

"All right," he said. "Sorry." He turned back to the ship's controls and stared at them. He heard her shoes stalk across the bridge and out the entry. Joe Chessman grunted sourly. Actually, Isobel Sanchez had a good deal of attraction for him, which he only partly laid to the fact that there were but two women in the ship's complement.

He heard a newcomer enter, and turned, even as a voice said, "Second watch reporting. Request permission to take over the bridge."

Chessman said, "Hello, Kennedy. You on already? Seems like I just got here." He muttered in self-contradiction. "Or that I've been here a month."

Technician Jerome Kennedy grinned. "Of course, if you want to stay..."

Chessman grunted scorn at that.

Kennedy said, "Wasn't that the Hot Pants Kid I just saw leaving?"

"That's right. All done up like a mopsy out looking for business."

Jerry Kennedy's grin was back again, even as he gave the control dials a quick, half-interested glance. "You can't say that about one of the women I love."

"One? Who's the other one?"

"Natalie, of course. Imagine, a year in space. Two good-looking women, sixteen men. You think we'll ever make it?"

Joe Chessman snorted. "That's why Mayer and Plekhanov made that ruling. No messing around. We'll make it."

Kennedy sank into one of the acceleration chairs before the control bank. "I think Leonid's sorry about that, now. Isobel's been giving him the sloe-eye bit."

Chessman snorted again. "Mayer's too old for her and Plekhanov's second in command."

"Come, come, Joe," Kennedy said in mock objection. "You don't think our consecrated leader would play favorites, just because some ambitious curve gave out a little."

Joe Chessman yawned and said, "I don't know about Plekhanov, but in the same position, I sure as Zen would."

Jerry Kennedy laughed.

Chessman said, "What're they doing in the lounge?"

Kennedy looked at the screen, not expecting to see anything and seeing just that. "Still on their endless argument."

Joe Chessman grunted.

Just to be saying something, Kennedy said, "How do you stand in the big debate?"

"I don't know. I suppose I favor Plekhanov. How we're going to take a bunch of savages and teach them modern agriculture and industrial methods in fifty years, using democratic institutions, I don't know. I can just see them putting it to a vote when we suggest fertilizer might be a good idea." He didn't feel like continuing the conversation. "See you later, Kennedy," and then, as an afterthought, formally, "Relinquishing the watch to Second Officer."

As he left the compartment, Jerry Kennedy called after him: "Hey, what's the course?"

Chessman growled over his shoulder. "The same it was last month, and the same it'll be next month." It wasn't much of a joke, but it was the only one they had between themselves.

In the ship's combination lounge and mess he drew a cup of coffee. Joe Chessman, among whose specialties were propaganda and primitive socio-economic systems, was third in line in the expedition's hierarchy. As such, he participated in the endless controversy dealing with overall strategy, but only as a junior member of the firm. Amschel Mayer and Leonid Plekhanov were the center of the fracas and right now were at it hot and heavy.

Joe Chessman listened with only half interest. He settled into a chair on the opposite side of the lounge and sipped at his coffee. They were going over their old battlefields, assaulting ramparts they'd stormed a thousand times over.

Plekhanov was saying doggedly: "Any planned economy is more efficient than any unplanned one. What could be more elementary than that? How could anyone in his right mind deny that?"

And Mayer snapped in high irritation. "*I* deny it. That term *planned economy* covers a multitude of sins. My dear Leonid, don't be an idiot..."

"I beg your pardon, sir!"

"Oh, don't get into one of your huffs, Plekhanov."

They were at that stage again.

Technician Natt Roberts entered, even here in the informality of space, looking as trim as a male fashion model. He had a book in hand and sent the trend of conversation in a new direction.

He said worriedly, "I've been studying up on this and what we're confronted with is two different ethnic periods—barbarism and feudalism. Handling them both at once doubles our problem."

Cogswell, an energetic junior specialist who'd been sitting to one side said, "That's not exactly sparkling new information, but I've been thinking about it too. And maybe I've got an answer. Why not all of us concentrate on Texcoco? When we've brought them up to the level of Genoa, which shouldn't take more than a decade or two, then we can start working on Genoa, too."

Mayer snapped, in a domineering voice. "And by that time we'll have hardly more than half our fifty years left to raise the two of them to an industrial technology. Don't be an idiot, Cogswell."

Cogswell flushed his resentment.

Plekhanov said slowly, "Besides, I'm not sure that, given the correct method, we cannot raise Texcoco to an industrialized society in approximately the same time it will take to bring Genoa there."

Mayer bleated a sarcastic laugh at that opinion.

Natt Roberts tossed his book to the table and sank into a chair. "If only one of them had maintained itself at a reasonable level of development, we'd have had help in working with the other. As it is, there are only eighteen of us." He shook his head. "Why did the knowledge held by the original colonists melt away? How can an intelligent people lose such basics as the smelting of iron, gunpowder, the use of coal as a fuel?"

Plekhanov was heavy with condescension. "Roberts, you seem to have entered upon this expedition with a lack of background. Consider: You put down a hundred colonists, products of the most advanced culture; among these you have one or two who can possibly repair an IBM computer, but is there one who can smelt iron or even locate the ore? We have others who could design an automated textile factory, but do any know how to weave a blanket on a hand loom?

"The first generation gets along well with the weapons and equipment brought with them from Earth. They maintain the old ways. The second generation follows along, but already ammunition for the weapons runs short, the machinery from Earth needs parts. There is no local economy that can provide such things. The third generation begins to think of Earth as a legend and the methods necessary to survive on the new planet conflict with those the first settlers imported. By the fourth generation, Earth is no longer a legend, but a fable..."

"But the books, the tapes, the films!" Roberts injected.

"Go with the guns, the vehicles and the other things brought from Earth. On a new planet there is no leisure class among the colonists. Each works hard if the group is to survive. There is no time to write new books, nor to copy the old, and the second and especially the third generation are impatient of the time needed to learn to read, time that should be spent in the fields or at the chase. The youth of an industrial culture can spend twenty years and more achieving a basic education before assuming adult responsibilities, but no pioneer society can afford to allow its offspring to so waste its time."

Natt Roberts was being stubborn. "But still, a few would carry the torch of knowledge."

Plekhanov added ponderously. "For a while. But then comes the reaction against these nonconformists, these crackpots who, by spending time at books, fail to carry their share of the load. One day they wake up to find themselves expelled from the group—if not knocked over the head."

Joe Chessman had been following Plekhanov's argument. He said dourly, "But finally the group conquers its environment to the point where a minimum of leisure is available again. Not for everybody, of course. The majority still have to spend their time from dawn till night plowing the fields, or watching the herds."

Amschel Mayer bounced back into the discussion. "And then, enter the priest, enter the war lord. Enter the smart operator who talks or fights himself into a position where he's free from drudgery. In short, enter the class-divided society, the rulers and the ruled."

Joe Chessman said reasonably, "If you don't have the man with leisure, society stagnates. Somebody has to have time off for thinking, if the whole group is to advance."

"Admittedly!" Mayer said. "I'd be the last to contend that an upper class is necessarily parasitic."

Plekhanov grumbled. "We're getting away from the subject. In spite of Mayer's poorly founded opinions, it is quite obvious that only a collectivized economy is going to enable these Rigel planets to achieve an industrial culture in as short a period as half a century."

Amschel Mayer reacted as might have been predicted. "Look here, Plekhanov, we have our own history to go by. Earth history. Man made his greatest strides under a freely competitive system."

"Well now..." Chessman began.

"Prove that!" Plekhanov insisted. "Your so-called free economy countries such as England, France and the United States began their industrial revolution in the early part of the nineteenth century. It took them a hundred years to accomplish what the Soviets did in fifty, in the next century."

"Just a *moment*, now," Mayer said. "That is very fine, but the Soviets were able to profit by the pioneering the free countries did. The scientific developments, the industrial techniques, were handed to her on a platter."

Specialist Martin Gunther, thus far quiet, as was his basic nature, put in his opinion. "Actually, it seems to me the fastest industrialization comes under a paternal guidance from a more advanced culture. Take Japan. In 1854 she was opened to trade by Commodore Perry. In 1871 she abolished feudalism and, encouraged by her own government and utilizing the most advanced techniques of a sympathetic West, she began to industrialize."

Gunther smiled his slow smile wryly. "Soon, to the dismay of the very countries that originally sponsored bringing her into the modern world, she was able to wage a successful war against China, and by 1904 she took on and trounced Russia. In a period of thirty-five years she had advanced from feudalism to a world power."

Joe Chessman took his turn. He said obdurately, "Your paternalistic guidance, given an uncontrolled competitive system, doesn't always work out. Take India after she gained independence from England. She tried to industrialize and had the support of the free nations. But what happened?"

Plekhanov leaned forward to take the ball. "Yes! There's your classic example. Compare India and China. China had a planned industrial development. None of this free competition nonsense. In ten years' time they had startled the world with their advances. In twenty years..."

"Yes," Gunther said softly, "but at what price?"

Plekhanov turned on him. "At any price! In one generation they left behind the China of famine, flood, illiteracy, war lords and all the misery that had been China's throughout history."

Gunther said mildly, "Whether or not, in their admitted advances, they left behind all the misery that had been China's is debatable, sir."

Plekhanov began to bellow an angry retort but Amschel Mayer popped suddenly to his feet and lifted a hand to quiet the others.

"Our solution has just come to me!"

Plekhanov glowered at him.

Mayer said excitedly, "Remember what the Co-ordinator told us? This expedition of ours is the first of its type. Even though we fail, the very mistakes we make will be invaluable. Our task is to learn how to bring backward peoples into an industrialized culture in roughly half a century."

He had their attention, but the majority of the occupants of the mess-room scowled at him. Thus far he had said nothing new.

Mayer went on enthusiastically. "Up until now, in our debates, we've had two basic suggestions on procedure. I have advocated a system of free competition; my learned colleague has been of the opinion that a strong state and a planned, not to say totalitarian economy, would be the quicker." He paused dramatically. "Very well, I am in favor of trying them both!"

They regarded him blankly.

He said with impatience, "There are two planets, at different ethnic periods it is true, but not so far apart as all that. Fine, nine of us will take Genoa and nine Texcoco."

Plekhanov rumbled, "Fine indeed. But which group will have the use of the *Pedagogue* with its library, its laboratories, its shops, its weapons?"

For a moment Mayer was stopped, but Joe Chessman growled, "That's no problem. Leave her in orbit around Rigel. We've got two small boats with which to ferry back and forth. Each group could have the use of her facilities any time they wished."

"I suppose we could have periodic conferences," Plekhanov said. "Say once every decade to compare notes and make further plans, if necessary."

Natt Roberts was worried. "We have no instructions from the Co-ordinator suggesting that we divide our forces in any such manner."

Mayer cut him short. "My dear Roberts, we were given *carte blanche*. It is up to us to decide procedure. Actually, this system realizes twice the information such expeditions as ours might ordinarily offer."

"Texcoco for me," Plekhanov grumbled, accepting the plan. "The more backward of the two, but under my guidance in half a century it will be the more advanced, mark me.

"Look here," Martin Gunther said. "Do we have two of each of the basic specialists, so that we can divide the party in such a way that neither planet will miss out in any one field?"

Amschel Mayer was beaming at the reception of his scheme. "The point is well taken, my dear Martin, however you'll recall that our training was deliberately made such that each man spreads over several fields. This in case, during our half century without contact with Earth, one or more of us meets with accident. Besides, the *Pedagogue*'s library is such that any literate can soon become effective in any field to the extent needed on the Rigel planets."

* * * *

Barry Watson met Natalie Wieliczka in a narrow corridor of the *Pedagogue*. He darted a look up and down the hallway, then held out his arms.

"Ho, Polack," he said huskily. "Come here."

She was apprehensive, but she came into his embrace and offered her mouth for his kiss.

She said, "Somebody might see us." After he had kissed her again, she said, "Barry, this is terrible. All this hiding, this pretending."

He grinned down into her open face. "Kind of fun, though," he said. "How lucky can a cloddy get?"

She said, "It's not fair. Everybody else is conforming to the command...."

"You sure?" he demanded, running his right hand up through her honey brown hair, cut short as befitted shipboard life. She was not an overly pretty girl, by most standards, but she had a gentle, serious sweetness that affected most men, though unbeknownst to herself.

She frowned slightly, even as she suffered his caresses. "How do you mean?"

"I suspect," he said wryly, "that these few kisses and hugs we allow ourselves at odd moments aren't nearly as serious as what your pal Isobel is dispensing to just about everybody in the team. Well, everybody but Mayer and myself."

She looked at him from the side of her eyes and said, "Are you sure you can honestly eliminate yourself?"

He squeezed her. "Absolutely."

She sighed, still in his arms. "However, I'll be glad when we reach Genoa, and this restriction will be off."

"Genoa?" He pushed her back to arm length and scowled down into her face.

"Why, yes, when we land and take up our work. Certainly, Amschel Mayer can have no objection then to our openly becoming married I... I wonder what ceremony they have. You know, when I was a student, sometimes thinking of marriage, I..."

"Genoa! But we're going to Texcoco."

Her eyes widened and there was quick apprehension in them.

"But Barry. I'm going to Genoa, with Mayer's team. I... why, I automatically thought you were as well. Everybody had a free choice. Surely, you couldn't have chosen Plekhanov's theories. Why..."

He took his hands from her completely, and tugged at his right ear in irritated distress.

"I was kind of pressured. I'm an authority on early military history. Leonid Plekhanov was of the opinion that I'd be more useful on Texcoco."

"Barry!" her voice was distressed now. "You could change. You could tell them you'd rather work on Genoa."

"Giving what excuse at this late date? The real one? The fact that you and I have broken ship's regulations and fallen in love?"

She looked at him in misery.

"Besides," he said angrily, "who'd change positions with me? Genoa is the preferred planet. It's more advanced. The life'll be easier. It'd be easier for you to change. Isobel's scheduled for Texcoco, but I have a sneaking suspicion that in spite of her supposed attraction to Plekhanov, she'd jump at the chance to switch to the Genoa team."

Her eyes dropped and she shook her head, and then shook it again, more strongly. "I couldn't, Barry, I couldn't work with that man. I'm afraid of him. All my intuition tells me that horrible things are going to happen on Texcoco, when Plekhanov and Joe Chessman land there with all the weapon resources of the *Pedagogue* behind them."

He said, bitterly, "Why not add me to the list? I'm the military expert. True enough, through books. I've never seen combat in my life. But who has, in this age? I've got the book knowledge but not the... practical experience."

She turned away from him, saying lowly, "You'll learn, Barry. You'll learn. And... I guess I'm just as glad I won't be seeing you doing the learning. I'm a doctor, Barry. I didn't go into my trade in anticipation of practicing on bodies broken in warfare."

He was exasperated, but she turned and moved slowly away in the direction she had been going when they met, her head down.

CHAPTER III

JOE CHESSMAN was at the controls of the space lighter. At his side sat Leonid Plekhanov and behind them the other seven members of their team, including Isobel Sanchez. They had circled Texcoco twice at great altitude, four times at a lesser one. Now they were low enough to spot a few man-made works.

"Nomadic," Plekhanov muttered. "Nomadic and village cultures."

"A few dozen urbanized cultures," Chessman said. "Whoever first compared the most advanced nation to the Aztecs was accurate, except for the fact that they base themselves along a river rather than on a mountain plateau."

Plekhanov said, "Similarities to the Egyptians and Sumerians, and the Indus valley culture of Mohenjo-Daro and Harappa—what Lewis Morgan would have called the latter stage of barbarism." He looked over his beefy shoulder at the technician who was photographing the areas over which they passed. "How does our geographer progress, Roberts?"

Natt Roberts brought his eyes up from his camera viewer. "I've got most of what we'll need for awhile, sir."

Isobel Sanchez said, "It's a beautiful world, Leonid."

Plekhanov ignored her use of his first name and turned back to Chessman. "We might as well head for their principle city, the one with the pyramids. We'll make initial contact there. I like the suggestion of surplus labor available."

"Surplus labor?" Chessman said, setting the controls. "How do you know?"

"Pryamids," Plekhanov rumbled. "I've always been of the opinion that such projects as pyramids, whether they be in Yucatan or Egypt, are make-work affairs. A priesthood, or other evolving ruling clique, keeping its people busy and out of mischief."

Chessman adjusted a speed lever and settled back. "I can see their point, keep the yokes busy and they don't have time to wonder why they, who do all the hard work, don't have the living standard of their betters."

"But I don't agree with it," Plekhanov said ponderously. "A society that builds pyramids is a static one. Both the Mayans and Egyptians are classic examples; for centuries, neither changed its basic culture. For that matter, any society that resorts to make-work projects to busy its citizenry has something basically wrong, and that includes the New Deal back in the Twentieth Century."

"Never heard of that one," Hawkins said, from his rear seat.

Joe Chessman said sourly, "I wasn't supporting the idea, just understanding the viewpoint of the priests. They'd made a nice thing for themselves and didn't want to see anything happen to it. It's not the only time a group in the saddle has held up progress for the sake of remaining there. Priests, slave owners, feudalistic barons, or bureaucrats of the Twentieth Century police states. A ruling clique will never give up power without pressure."

Barry Watson leaned forward and pointed down and to the right. "There's the river," he said. "And there's their capital city. Whoever selected its location didn't have much of an eye for defense."

"It probably wasn't selected," Chessman said. "It probably just evolved there from some original watering place, or trade crossroads."

The small spacecraft settled at decreasing speed.

Chessman said, "The central square? It seems to be their market, by the number of people."

"I suppose so," Plekhanov said. "Right there before the largest pyramid. We'll remain inside the craft for the rest of today and tonight."

Isobel said, her voice low, "But good heavens, that's going to be awfully... intimate. Me in here with you eight men."

Natt Roberts, who had put away his camera, backed her. "Yes, why? Doctor Sanchez is right. It's too crowded in here."

"Because I said so," Plekhanov rumbled. "This first impression is important. Our flying machine is undoubtedly the first they've seen. We've got to give them time to get used to the idea and then get together a welcoming committee. We'll want the top men, right from the beginning."

"The equivalent of the Emperor Montezuma meeting Cortez, eh?" Barry Watson said. "A real red carpet welcome."

The *Pedagogue*'s space lighter settled to the plaza gently, some fifty yards from the ornate pyramid which stretched up over a hundred and fifty feet and was topped by a small, templelike building. It could have been the twin of the so-called House of the Magician in Uxmal, Yucatan.

Chessman stretched and stood up from the controls. "Your anthropology ought to be better than that, Barry," he said. "There was no Emperor Montezuma and no Aztec Empire, except in the minds of the Spaniards." He peered out one of the heavy ports. "And by the looks of this town, we'll find a duplicate of Aztec society. I don't believe they've even got the wheel."

21

The nine of them clustered about the craft's portholes, taking in the city that surrounded them. The square had emptied magically at their approach, and now the several thousand citizens that had filled it were peering fearfully from street entrances and alleyways.

Isobel Sanchez, pressed up against the side of Plekhanov, said, "Look at the manner in which the women utilize feathers in their costume."

Plekhanov grunted. "As our doctor, my dear, I would have expected you to have first noted their stature. It indicates a high protein diet, and since the area isn't particularly suited to the chase, that in turn would indicate extensive herds. I would suspect they are an aggressive people, rather than just sedentary farmers huddled behind their city walls."

Cogswell, the technician, said, "Look at them! It'll take hours before they drum up enough courage to come any closer. You were right, Doctor Plekhanov. If we left the boat now, we'd make fools of ourselves trying to coax them near enough to talk."

Watson said to Joe Chessman, "What do you mean, no Emperor Montezuma? I know *that* much history."

Chessman said absently, as he stared out at the primitive city, "When the Spanish got to Mexico, they didn't understand what they saw, being musclemen rather than scholars. And before competent witnesses came on the scene, Aztec society was destroyed. The *conquistadores* who did attempt to describe Tenochtitlan, misinterpreted it. They were from a feudalistic world and tried to portray the Aztecs in such terms. For instance, the large Indian community houses they thought were palaces. Actually, Montezuma was a democratically elected war-chief of a confederation of three tribes which dominated the Mexican valley. There was no empire because Indian society, being based on the clan, had no method of assimilating newcomers. The Aztec armies could loot and they could capture prisoners for their sacrifices, but they had no system of bringing their conquered enemies into the nation. They hadn't reached that far in the evolution of society. The Incas could have taught them a few lessons."

Plekhanov nodded. "Besides, the Spanish were fabulous liars. In Cortez's attempt to impress Spain's king, he built himself up far beyond reality. To read his reports you'd think the pueblo of Mexico had a population pushing a million. Actually, if it had thirty thousand, it was doing well. Without a field agriculture and with their primitive transport, they must have been hard put to feed even that large a town."

A tall, erect native strode from one of the streets and approached to within twenty feet of the spacecraft. He stared at it for at least ten full minutes, then spun on his heel and strode off again in the direction of one of the stolidly built stone buildings that lined the square on each side except that which the pyramid dominated.

Cogswell said, "Now that he's broken the ice, in a couple of hours kids will be scratching their names on our hull."

* * * *

In the morning, two or three hours after dawn, they made their preparations to disembark. Of them all, only Leonid Plekhanov was unarmed. Joe Chessman had a heavy handgun holstered at his waist. The rest of the men carried submachine guns; Isobel Sanchez had a small automatic. More destructive weapons were hardly called for, nor available for that matter; once world government had been established on Earth the age-old race for improved arms had fallen away.

Chessman assumed active command of the group, growling brief instructions.

"If there's any difficulty, remember we're civilizing a planet of nearly a billion population. The life or death of a few individuals is meaningless. Look at our position scientifically, dispassionately. If it becomes necessary to use force—we have the right, and the might to back it up. MacBride, you stay with the ship. Keep the hatch closed and station yourself at the gun. I'd leave Doctor Sanchez, but I doubt if she could buck that heavy a weapon."

MacBride, a dour-faced specialist, was unhappy about being left behind at this historic moment, but said nothing. Each individual in the group fully realized the present need of exact discipline.

The natives seemed to know intuitively that the occupants of the craft from the sky would present themselves at this time. Several thousands of them crowded the plaza. Warriors armed with spears and bronze headed warclubs, kept the more adventurous from crowding too near.

The hatch opened, the steel landing ramp snaked out, and the hefty Plekhanov stepped down, closely followed by Chessman. The others brought up the rear: Watson, Roberts, Stevens, Hawkins, Cogswell, and finally Isobel Sanchez. They had hardly formed a compact group at the foot of the spacecraft than the ranks of the natives parted and what was obviously a delegation of officials approached them. In the fore was a giant of a man in his late middle years, and at his side, a cold visaged duplicate of him, obviously a son.

Behind these were variously dressed others—military, priesthood, local officials, by their appearance. They made a brave show in their barbaric splendor, bright with color and spectacular design. Gold and gems decorated costume and weapons of all save the priesthood who were, as so often in a priesthood, garbed in black.

Ten feet from the newcomers they stopped. The leader said in quiet understandable Amer-English, "I am Taller, Khan of all the People. Our legends tell of you. You must be from First Earth." He added with a simple

23

dignity, a quiet gesture, "Welcome to the World. Come in Peace and find Peace. How may we serve you?"

Plekhanov looked at the other for a long thoughtful moment, then took his approach.

He said flatly, "The name of this planet is Texcoco and the inhabitants shall henceforth be called Texcocans. You are correct, we have come from Earth. Our instructions are to civilize you, to bring you the latest technology, to prepare you to enter the community of planets, the Galactic Commonwealth."

Phlegmatically he let his eyes go to the pyramids, to the temples, and the large community dwelling quarters. "We'll call this city Tula, and its citizens Tulans."

Taller took his turn at looking thoughtful, not having missed the tone of arrogant command.

One of the group behind the Khan, clad in flowing black robes, said to Plekhanov, mild reproof in his voice, "My son, we are the most advanced folk on... Texcoco. We have thought of ourselves as civilized. However, we..."

Plekhanov rumbled, "I am not your son, old man, and you are far short of civilization. We can't stand here forever. Take us to a building where we can talk without these crowds staring at us. There is much to be done."

Taller, the Khan, said, "This is Mynor, Chief Priest of the People."

The priest bowed his head, then said, "The People are used to and expect ceremony on outstanding occasions. We have arranged for suitable sacrifices to the gods. At their completion, we will proclaim a festival. And then—"

The warriors had cleared a way through the multitude to the base of the pyramid which reared steep above them. And now the Earthlings could see a score of chained men and women, nude save for loin cloths and fetters, and obviously captives.

Plekhanov glared at Taller. "You were going to kill these?"

The Khan said reasonably, "They are not of the People. They are prisoners taken in battle."

Mynor said, "Their lives please the gods."

"There are no gods, as you probably know," Plekhanov said flatly. "You will no longer sacrifice prisoners."

A hush fell over the Texcocans near enough to hear his words. Joe Chessman let his hand drop to his weapon. The movement was not lost on Taller's son, whose eyes narrowed.

"Leonid, Joe," Isobel Sanchez murmured anxiously.

The Khan looked at the burly Plekhanov for a long moment. He said slowly, "Our institutions fit our needs. What would you have us do with these people? They are our enemies. If we turn them loose, they will fight us again. If we keep them imprisoned, they will eat our food. We... Tulans are not poor, we have food aplenty, for we Tulans, but we cannot feed all the thousands of prisoners we take in our wars."

He hesitated a moment, then went on. "In the far past, our legends tell us, prisoners were eaten. Indeed, some of the more backwards peoples of... Texcoco, still so treat their prisoners. But we are not so primitive. We sacrifice them to the gods. What would you have us do with them?"

Joe Chessman said dryly, "As of today, there is a new policy. We put them to work."

Plekhanov rumbled at him. "I'll explain our position, Chessman, if you please." Then to the Tulans. "To develop this planet, we're going to need the labor of every man, woman and child capable of work."

Taller said, after considering, "Perhaps your suggestion that we retire to a less public place is desirable. Will you follow?" He spoke a few words to an officer of the warriors, who shouted orders.

The Khan led the way with considerable dignity. Plekhanov and Chessman followed, side by side, and the other Earthlings brought up the rear of the leading group, their weapons at the ready. Following this group were Mynor, the priest, his face in a worried scowl, Taller's son, and the other Tulan officials.

In what was evidently the reception hall of Taller's official residence, the newcomers were made as comfortable as fur padded low stools permitted. Half a dozen teenage Tulans brought a cool drink somewhat similar to cocoa; it seemed to give a slight, though not quite alcoholic, lift.

Taller had not become Khan of the most progressive nation on Texcoco by other than his own abilities. The office was elective. He felt his way carefully now. He had no manner of knowing the powers wielded by these strangers from space. He suspected they were considerable and had no intention of precipitating a situation in which he would discover such powers to his sorrow.

He said carefully, "You have indicated that you intend major changes in the lives of the People."

"Of all Texcocans," Plekhanov said. "You Tulans are merely the beginning."

Mynor, the aged priest, leaned forward. "But why? We do not wish these changes—whatever they may be. Already the Khan has allowed you to interfere with our worship of our gods. This will mean—"

Plekhanov growled, "Be silent, old man, and don't bother to mention, ever again, your so-called gods. Gods have ever been the invention of men, to keep in suppression their fellow men. And now, all of you listen.

Perhaps some of this will not be new. How much history has come down to you, I don't know.

"A thousand years ago, a colony of one hundred persons was left here on Texcoco. It will one day be of scholarly interest to trace them down through the centuries, but at present the task does not interest us. This expedition has been sent to recontact you, now that you have populated Texcoco and made such adaptations as were necessary to survive here. Our basic task is to modernize your society, to bring it to an industrialized culture."

Plekhanov's eyes went to Taller's son. "I assume you are a soldier?"

Taller said, "This is Reif, my eldest, and by our custom, second in command of the People's armies. As Khan, I am first."

Reif nodded coldly to Plekhanov. "I am a soldier." He hesitated for a moment, then added, "And willing to die to protect the People."

"Indeed," Plekhanov rumbled. "As a soldier you will be interested to know that our first step will involve the uniting of all the nations and tribes of this planet. Not a small task. There should be opportunity for you."

Taller said, "Surely you speak in jest. The People have been at war for as long as scribes have records and never have we been stronger than today, never larger. But to conquer the world! Surely you jest."

Plekhanov grunted ungraciously. He looked over at the lanky Barry Watson, a seeming youth, now leaning negligently against the wall, his submachine gun, however, at the easy ready. "Watson, you're our military expert. Have you any opinions as yet?"

"Yes, sir," Watson said. "Until we can get iron weapons and firearms into full production, I suggest the phalanx for their infantry. They have the horse, but the wheel seems to have gone out of use. We'll introduce the chariot and also heavy carts to speed up logistics. We'll bring in the saddle too, for better lance action. I have available for study the works of every cavalry leader from Tamerlane to Jeb Stuart. Yes, sir, I have some ideas."

Plekhanov pursed his heavy lips. "From the beginning we're going to need manpower on a scale never dreamed of locally. We'll adapt a policy of expansion. Those who join us freely will become members of the State with full privileges. Those who resist will be made prisoners of war and used for shock labor on the roads and in the mines. However, a man works better if he has a goal, a dream. Each prisoner will be freed and become a member of the State after ten years of such work."

He turned to his subordinates. "Roberts and Hawkins, you will begin tomorrow to seek the nearest practical sources of iron ore and coal. Wherever you discover them, we'll direct our first military expeditions. Chessman and Cogswell, you'll assemble their best artisans and begin their training in such basic advancements as the wheel."

He looked to Isobel Sanchez. "Doctor Sanchez, you'll immediately establish a hospital and laboratory and begin such advancements as the introduction of the antibiotics."

"Yes, Leonid," Isobel said.

Taller said softly, "You speak of advancement, but thus far you have mentioned largely war and on such a scale that I wonder how many of the People will survive. What advancement? We have all we wish."

Plekhanov cut him off with a curt motion of his hand. He indicated the symbols inscribed on the chamber's walls. "How long does it take to learn such writing?"

Mynor, the priest, said, "This is a mystery known only to the priesthood. One spends ten years in preparation to be a scribe."

"We'll teach you a new method which will have every citizen of the State reading and writing within a year."

The Tulans gaped at him.

Mynor said, in protest, "But writing is only permitted of priests."

Plekhanov ignored him. He moved ponderously over to Roberts, drew from its scabbard the sword the other had on his hip. He took it and slashed savagely at a stone post, gouging a heavy chunk from it. He tossed the weapon to Reif, whose eyes lit up.

"What metals have you been using? Copper, bronze? You're going to move into the iron age overnight."

He turned to Taller. "Are your priests also in charge of the health of your people?" he sneered. "Are their cures obtained from mumbo-jumbo and few herbs found in the desert? Doctor Sanchez has at her command the most advanced medical methods. Within a decade, I'll guarantee you that not one of your major diseases will remain."

He turned to the priest and said, "Or perhaps this will be the clincher for some of you. How many years do you have, *old man?*"

Mynor said with dignity, "I am sixty-four."

Plekhanov said churlishly, "And I am two hundred and thirty-three." He called to Hawkins. "I think you're our youngest. How old are you, Dick?"

Dick Hawkins grinned. "Hundred and thirteen, next month."

Mynor opened his mouth, closed it again. No man would prolong his youth. Of a sudden he felt old, old.

Young Reif, the Khan's son, looked at Isobel Sanchez, his eyes wide. They went up and down her figure, outlined even through the coveralls she wore. He blinked. She smiled back at him, maliciously, and her dark eyes went up and down his own masculine figure. He blinked again.

Plekhanov turned back to Taller. "Most of the progress we have to offer is beyond your capacity to understand. We'll give you freedom from want. Health. We'll give you advances in every art. We'll eventually free every citizen from drudgery, educate him, give him the opportunity to enjoy intellectual curiosity. We'll open the stars to him. All these things the coming of the State will eventually mean to you."

Tula's Khan was not impressed. "This you tell us, man from First Earth. But to achieve these you plan to change every phase of our lives and we are happy with... Tula... the way it is. I say this to you. There are but eight of you, and one woman. And there are many, many of us. We do not want your... State. Return from whence you came."

Plekhanov shook his massive head at the other. "Whether or not *you* want these changes, they will be made. If you fail to cooperate, we will find someone who will. I suggest you make the most of it."

Taller arose from the squat stool upon which he had been seated. He was no coward. "I have listened and I do not like what you have said. I am Khan of all the People. Now leave in peace, or I shall order my warriors..."

"Joe," Plekhanov said flatly. "Watson!"

Joe Chessman took his heavy handgun from its holster and triggered it twice. The roar of the explosions reverberated thunderously in the confined space, deafening all, and terrifying the Tulans. Bright red colored the robes the Khan wore, colored them without beauty. Bright red splattered the floor.

Leonid Plekhanov stared at his second in command, wet his thick lips. "Joe," he sputtered. "I hadn't... I didn't expect you to be so... hasty."

Joe Chessman, his gun still at the ready, growled: "We've got to let them know where we stand, right now, or they'll never hold still for us. Cover the doors, Watson, Roberts." He motioned to the others with his head. "Cogswell, Hawkins, Stevens, get to those windows and watch."

Taller was a crumbled heap on the floor. The other Texcocans stared at his body in shocked horror.

Isobel had sunk down beside the Khan. She looked up, now, a shine in her eyes, but her face otherwise empty. She looked at Chessman and said, "The man is dead."

"Of course," Chessman said, his gun still at the ready and staring at Reif.

The Khan's son sank down beside his father, too. He looked up, his lips white, at Plekhanov. "Yes, he is dead."

Leonid Plekhanov collected himself. "It was his own fault."

Reif's cold face was expressionless. He looked at Joe Chessman. He said, "You can supply such weapons to my armies?"

Plekhanov said, "That is our intention, in time."

Reif came erect. "Subject to the approval of the clan leaders, I am now Khan. Tell me more of this State of which you have spoken."

CHAPTER IV

THE SERGEANT stopped the small company about a quarter of a mile from the city of Bari. His detachment numbered only ten but they were well armed with swords and blunderbusses and wore mail and iron helmets. On the face of it, they would have been a match for ten times this number of merchants.

It was hardly noon, but the sergeant had already been at his wine flask. He leered at them. "And where do you think you go?"

The merchant who led the rest was a thin little man but he was richly robed and astride a heavy black mule. He said, "To Bari, soldier."

He drew a paper from a pouch. "I hold this permission from Baron Mannerheim to pass through his lands with my people."

The leer turned mercenary. "Unfortunately, city man, I can't read. What do you carry on the mules and asses?"

"Personal property which, I repeat, I have permission to transport through Baron Mannerheim's lands free of charge and worry from his followers." He added in irritation, "The Baron is a friend of mine, fond of the gifts I give him. Only last week, we supped together."

One of the soldiers grunted his skepticism, checked the flint on the lock of his piece, then looked at the sergeant suggestively.

The sergeant said, "As you say, merchant, my lord the baron is fond of gifts. But aren't we all? Unfortunately, I have received no word of your passage. My instructions are to stop all intruders upon the baron's lands and, if there is resistance, to slay them and confiscate such properties as they may be carrying."

The merchant sighed and reached into his pouch again. The eyes of the sergeant dropped in greed. The hand emerged with two small coins. "As you say," the merchant muttered bitterly, "we are all fond of gifts. Will you accept this and do me the honor to drink my health at the tavern tonight?"

The sergeant's mouth slackened and he fondled the hilt of his sword.

"Do you insult me by offering me a bribe, merchant?" He cleared his throat suggestively. "Such a small bribe, at that?"

The merchant sighed again and dipped into the pouch. This time his hand emerged with half a dozen bits of silver. He handed them down to the other, complaining, "How can a man profit in his affairs if every few miles he must pass another outstretched hand?"

The sergeant growled. "You do not seem to starve, city man. Now, on your way. You are fortunate I am too lazy today to bother going through your things. Besides," and he grinned widely, "the baron gave me personal instructions not to bother you."

The merchant snorted, kicked his heels into his beast's sides and led his half dozen followers toward the city. The soldiers looked after them and howled their amusement. The money was enough to keep them drunk for days.

When they were out of earshot, Amschel Mayer grinned his amusement back over his shoulder at Jerome Kennedy. "How'd that come off, Jerry?"

The other sniffed in mock deprecation. "You're beginning to fit into the local merchant pattern better than the real thing. However, just for the record, I had this, ah, grease gun, trained on them all the time."

Amschel Mayer said, "Only in extreme emergency, my dear Jerry. The baron would be up in arms if he found a dozen of his men massacred on the outskirts of Bari, and we don't want a showdown at this stage. It's taken nearly a year to build this part we act."

At this time of day the gates of the port city of Bari were open and the guards lounged idly. Their captain recognized Amschel Mayer and did no more than nod respectfully. The merchant and his party proceeded through the heavy stone gate, with its grill of iron, now lifted, its ultrathick, ironstudded doors open behind.

Jerry Kennedy said from the side of his mouth, "A couple of sticks of dynamite and you'd have a hole you could march a regiment through."

And Mayer answered placidly, "Which is one of the reasons we have not as yet introduced dynamite, my dear Jerry." He kicked his heels into his mount's sides.

They wended their way through narrow, cobblestoned streets, avoiding the crowds in the central market area. They pulled up eventually before a house both larger and more ornate than its neighbors. Mayer and Kennedy dismounted from the horses and left their care to the others.

Amschel Mayer beat the heavy knocker on the door and a slot opened for a quick check of his identity. The door opened wide and technician Martin Gunther let them in.

"The others are here already?" Mayer asked him.

Gunther nodded. "Since breakfast. Baron Leonar, in particular, is impatient."

Mayer was proceeding down the tapestry-hung, still grim, hall. He said over his shoulder, "All right, Jerry, get the servants to bring that stuff in.

This is where we put it to them. Or, as the old expression had it, lay it on the line."

Followed by Martin Gunther, he entered the long conference room. A full score of men sat around the heavy wooden table. Most of them were as richly garbed as their host. Most of them were in their middle years. All of them were alert of eye. All of them confidently at ease. They were men of strength, no matter their physical make-up, which varied considerably.

Amschel Mayer took his place at the table's end, and took the time to speak to each of his guests individually. By the termination of that, Jerome Kennedy had entered the room and sank into the chair next to him.

Mayer leaned back and took in the gathering as a whole. He said, "You probably realize that this group consists of the twenty most powerful merchants on the continent."

The one he had greeted earlier as Olderman, nodded. "We have been discussing your purpose in bringing us together, Honorable Mayer All of us are not friends." He twisted his face in amusement. "In fact, very few of us are friends. Competition, when one reaches our level, does not bring with it personal regard."

"There is no need for you to be," Mayer said. "But all are going to realize the need for cooperation. Honorables, I have just come from the city of Ronda, where I needed the help of some of the artisans there to complete my preparations for this meeting. Although I had paid heavily in advance to the three barons whose lands I crossed, I had to bribe myself through a dozen roadblocks, had to pay fabulous rates to cross three ferries, and once had to fight off supposed bandits."

One of his guests grumbled, "Who were actually probably soldiers of the local baron who decided that although you paid him transit fee, it still might be profitable to go through your goods."

Mayer nodded. "Exactly, my dear Honorable, and that is why we've gathered."

Olderman had evidently assumed spokesmanship for the others. Now he said warily, "I don't believe I quite understand, Honorable Mayer. Your urgent invitation that I attend this conference suggested that it would be greatly to my profit. It is for this reason I am here."

Mayer suppressed his characteristic impatience. "Genoa, if you'll pardon the use of this name to signify the world upon which we reside, will never advance until trade has been freed from these bandits who call themselves lords and barons."

Eyebrows reached for hairlines.

Olderman's eyes went quickly about the room, went to the doors. "Please," he said. "The servants."

"My servants are safe," Mayer said.

However, several of his guests stirred in their chairs unhappily.

One of them was smiling without humor. "You seem to forget, Honorable Mayer, that I carry the title of baron."

Amschel Mayer shook his head. "No, Baron Leonar. But neither do you disagree basically with what I say. The businessman, the merchant, the manufacturer on Genoa today, is only tolerated. He is a second-rate citizen of middle class. Were it not for the fact that the barons have no desire to eliminate such a profitable source of income, they would milk us dry overnight."

Someone shrugged. "That is the way of things. We are fortunate to have wrested, bribed and begged as many favors and privileges from the lords as we have. Our twenty cities all have charters that protect us from complete ruin."

"So long as they wish to continue to observe the charters," Mayer snorted. "A whim might decide the Baron Mannerheim tomorrow to march on Bari. A sizeable donation to the Temple would guarantee its blessing, and the charter would be put aside, legally, on some obscure technicality."

One of the guests said, "That is indeed possible. But what is your point, Honorable?"

Mayer twisted with a small boy's excitement in his chair. "As of today, things begin to change. Jerry, that press."

Jerry Kennedy left the room momentarily and returned with Martin Gunther and two of the servants. While the assembled merchants looked on, in puzzled silence, Mayer's assistants set up the press and a stand holding two fonts of fourteen point type.

Jerry took up a printer's stick and gave running instructions and description as he demonstrated. Gunther handed around pieces of the type until all had examined it, while his colleague set up several lines.

Kennedy transposed the lines to a chase, locked it up and placed the form to one side while he demonstrated inking the small press, which was operated by a foot pedal. He mounted the form in the press, took a score of sheets of paper and rapidly fed them, one by one with his right hand, removing them with his left. When they were all printed, he stopped pumping and Gunther handed the still wet, finished product around to the mystified audience.

Olderman stared down at the printed lines, scowling in concentration. He wet his lips in sudden comprehension.

But it was merchant Russ who blurted, "This will revolutionize the inscribing of books. Why, it can well take it out of the hands of the Temple! With such a machine I could make a hundred books—"

Mayer was beaming. "Not a hundred, Honorable, but a hundred thousand!"

The others stared at him as though he were demented. "A hundred thousand," one said. "There are not that many literate persons on the continent."

"There will be," Mayer crowed. "This is but one of our levers to pry power from the barons. And here is another." He tuned to Russ. "Honorable Russ, your city is noted for the fine quality of its steel, of the swords and armor you produce."

Russ nodded. He was a small man, fantastically rich in his attire. "This is true, Honorable Mayer."

Mayer said, tossing a small booklet to the other. "I have here the plans for a new method of making steel from pig iron. The principle involved is the oxidation of the impurities in the iron by blowing air through the molten metal."

Amschel Mayer turned to still another, "And your town is noted for its fine textiles." He looked to his assistants. "Jerry, you and Gunther bring in those models of the power loom and the spinning jenny."

While they were gone, he said, "My intention is to assist you to speed up production. With this in mind, you'll appreciate the automatic flying shuttle that we'll now demonstrate."

Kennedy and Gunther re-entered accompanied by four servants and a mass of equipment. Kennedy muttered to Amschel Mayer, "I feel like the instructor of a handicraft class."

Half an hour later, Kennedy and Gunther wound up passing out pamphlets to the awed merchant guests. Kennedy said, "This booklet will give details on construction of the equipment and its operation."

Mayer pursed his lips. "Your people will be able to assimilate only so fast, so we won't push them. Later, you'll be interested in introducing the mule spinning frame, among other items."

He motioned for the servants to remove the printing press and textile machinery. "We now come to probably the most important of the devices I have to introduce to you today. Because of its size and weight, I've had constructed only a model. Jerry!"

Jerry Kennedy brought to the heavy table a small steam engine. He had half a dozen attachments for it. Within moments he had the others around him, as enthusiastic as a group of youngsters with a new toy.

"By the Supreme," Baron Leonar blurted, "do you realize this device could be used instead of waterpower to operate a mill, to power the loom demonstrated half an hour ago?"

Honorable Russ was rubbing the side of his face thoughtfully. "It might even be adapted to move a coach. A coach without horses. Unbelievable!"

Mayer chuckled in pleased excitement and clapped his hands. A servant entered with a toy wagon which had been slightly altered. Martin Gunther lifted the small engine, placed it in position atop the wagon, connected it quickly and threw a lever. The wagon moved smoothly forward, the first car of Genoa's industrial revolution.

Martin Gunther smiled widely at Russ. "You mean like this, Honorable?"

Half an hour later, they were reseated, before each of them a small pile of instructions, plans, blueprints.

Mayer said, "I have one more device to bring to your attention at this time. Perhaps I wish it were unnecessary but I am afraid otherwise."

He held up for their inspection, a bullet. Jerry Kennedy handed around samples to the merchants. They fingered them in puzzlement.

"Honorables," Mayer said. "The barons have the use of gunpowder. Muskets and muzzleloading cannon are available to them both for their wars against each other and their occasional attacks upon our supposedly independent chartered cities. However, this is an advancement on their weapons. This unit includes not only the lead of the bullet, but the powder and the cap which will explode it."

They lacked understanding, and showed it.

Mayer said, "Jerry, if you'll demonstrate."

Jerry Kennedy said, "The bullet can be adapted to various weapons, however, this is one of the simplest." He pressed, one after another, a full twenty rounds into his gun's clip.

"Now if you'll note the silhouette of a man I've drawn on the wooden frame at the end of the room." He pressed the trigger, sending a single shot into the figure.

Olderman nodded. "An improvement in firearms. But—"

Kennedy said, "However, if you are confronted with more than one of the bad guys." He grinned and flicked the gun over to full automatic and in a Götterdämmerung of sound in the confines of the room, emptied the clip into his target, sending splinters and chips flying and all but demolishing the wooden backdrop.

His audience sat back in stunned horror at the demonstration.

Mayer said, "The weapon is simple to construct. Any competent gunsmith can do it. It is manifest, Honorables, that with your people so armed your cities will be safe from attack and so will trading caravans and ships."

Russ said shakily, "Your intention is good, Honorable Mayer, however it will be but a matter of time before the barons will have solved the secrets of your weapons. Such cannot be withheld forever. Then we would again be at their mercy."

"Believe me, Honorable," Mayer said dryly, "by that time I will have new weapons to introduce, if necessary. Weapons that make this one a very toy in comparison."

Olderman resumed his office as spokesman. "This demonstration has astounded us, Honorable Mayer, but although we admire your abilities, it need hardly be pointed out that it seems unlikely all this could be the product of one brain."

"They are not mine," Mayer admitted. "They are the products of many minds."

"But where—?"

The Earthman shook his head. "I don't believe I will tell you now."

"I see." The Genoese eyed him emotionlessly. "Then the question becomes, *why?*"

Mayer said, carefully now, "It may be difficult for you to see, but the introduction of each of these will be a nail in feudalism's coffin. Each will increase either production or trade and such increase will lead to the overthrow of feudal society."

Baron Leonar, who had remained largely silent throughout the afternoon, now spoke up. "As you said earlier, although I am a titled lord myself, my interests are your own. I am a merchant first. However, I am not sure I want the changes these devices will bring. Frankly, Honorable Mayer, I am satisfied with my world as I find it today."

There was at least one murmur of approval from the merchants who sat about the table.

Amschel Mayer smiled wryly at the other. "I am afraid you *must* adapt to these new developments."

The baron said coldly, "Why? I do not like to be told I must do something. I am an important figure in the world as I know it. Radical change may upset this. If we loose these devices upon the world—Genoa, as you call it—who can say who will fall from the heights, and who will climb up from below? The status quo is always the safest for those on top."

Mayer nodded acceptance of that. "Because, my dear baron, there are three continents on the planet of Genoa. At present, there is little trade due to infrequent shipping. But the steam engine I introduced today will soon drive larger craft than you have ever built before."

Russ said, "What has this to do with our being forced to use these devices? I find much to cause me halt in what Baron Leonar has said."

"I have colleagues on the other continents busily introducing the same inventions, Honorable. If you don't adapt, in time, competitors will invade your markets, capture your trade, drive you out of business."

Mayer wrapped it up. "Honorables, modernize or go under. It's each man for himself and the devil take the hindmost, if you'll allow a saying from another era."

Kennedy added, grinning, "Sometimes known as free enterprise."

They remained silent for a long period. Finally Olderman said bluntly, "The barons are not going to like this."

The usually quiet Martin Gunther said softly, "Obviously, that is why we have introduced you to the tommy gun. It is not going to make any difference if they like it or not."

Russ said musingly; "Pressure will be put to prevent the introduction of this equipment. It will obviously upset society."

"We'll meet it," Mayer said, shifting happily in his seat.

Russ added, "The Temple's ever on the side of the barons. The monks will fight against innovations that threaten to disturb the present way of things."

Mayer said, "Monks usually do. How much property is in the hands of the Temple?"

Russ admitted sourly, "The monks are the greatest landlords of all. I would say at least one-third of the land and the serfs belong to the Temple."

"Ah ha," Mayer said thoughtfully. "That bears some further looking into. We must investigate the possibilities of a Reformation. But that can come later. Now I wish to expand upon my reasons for gathering you.

"Honorables, Genoa is to change rapidly. To survive, you will have to move fast. I have not introduced these revolutionary changes without self interest. Each of you is free to use them to his profit, however, I expect a thirty percent interest."

There was a universal drawing in of breath.

Olderman said, "Honorable Mayer, you have already demonstrated your devices. What is there to prevent us from playing you false?"

Mayer laughed. "My dear Olderman, I have other inventions to reveal as rapidly as you develop the technicians, the workers capable of building and operating them. If you cheat me now, you will be passed by next time."

Russ muttered. "Thirty percent! Your wealth will be unbelievable."

"As fast as it accumulates, Honorables, it shall be invested. For instance, I have great interest in expanding our inadequate universities. The advance I expect will only be possible if we educate the people. Field serfs are not capable of running even that simple steam engine Jerry demonstrated."

Baron Leonar said, "What you contemplate is mind shaking. Do I understand that you wish a confederation of all our cities? A joining together to combat the strength of the present lords and of the Temple?"

Mayer was shaking his head. "No, no. As the barons lose power, each of your cities will strengthen and possibly expand to become nations. Perhaps some will unite. But largely you will compete against each other and against the nations of the other continents. In such competition you'll have to show your mettle, or go under. Man develops at his fastest when pushed by such circumstances."

The Earthling looked off, unseeing, into a far corner of the room. "At least, so is my contention. Far away from here, a colleague is attempting to prove me wrong. We shall see."

CHAPTER V

BARRY WATSON was dressed in the leather kilts and fatigue jacket of the Tulan non-com. Except for the heavy hand gun, slung low on his hip, he was indistinguishable from the drill sergeants who sweated and swore in the mid-day sun. Looking nothing so much as a lanky youngster, he sauntered up, checking a sheaf of reports as he came.

Terry Stevens, still attired in the coveralls that had been standard garb on the spaceship *Pedagogue*, called an order to one of his sergeants, who, as sergeants ever, barked out a command that could be heard from one end of the drill field to the other. The shuffling footmen came to a halt, fell into an at ease stance.

Barry Watson looked out over the field. The men were dressed in fatigues, the weapons they carried were of wood, the shields were light frameworks covered with cloth.

Barry said, "How're they coming, Terry?"

Stevens grunted and wiped the back of his hand over his mouth. "All right, I suppose. This isn't exactly my game, you know. They start out stumbling all over their feet, get their spears stuck between their legs. That goes on for weeks. They don't seem to learn anything. Then, all of a sudden, the whole cohort is moving like a machine. They're doing all right."

Watson looked down at his reports. "This gang should've been ready for campaigning a couple of weeks ago. They should be in the field by now."

Stevens said defensively, "I'm not as up on this as you are, Barry. It's not my line."

"It's not my line, either. Only out of books. We're all playing it more or less by ear. We're lucky we're not trying to train really well drilled men. The phalanx was originally conceived to take peasants, arm them simply and send them into action with a minimum of training."

"Well, if all this is what you call a minimum of training, I'd hate to have to go through getting them into real trim."

Barry chuckled. "Well, things have developed. A Theban named Epaminondas figured out some new departures. His innovations were so acute that they were continued and utilized as late as Frederick the Great."

"I thought this was all based on the Greeks," Stevens said, not really interested.

"The Macedonians. Philip came along, learned all that the Thebans knew about the phalanx and added some contributions of his own, particularly the use of cavalry in conjunction with the foot."

Stevens snorted. "You want to know something? Back at the university, they used to call me the last of the pacifists."

Barry Watson looked at him.

Stevens chuckled. "We used to have debates on whether or not the military should be tolerated on the newly opening planets."

"And what did you decide?"

"Nothing. What's ever decided by debating?"

Barry Watson turned to one of the drill sergeants. "Let's put them through open phalanx to tortuga, sergeant."

The non-com Tulan came to the salute. "Yes, sir." He wheeled about sharply and barked out an order.

The men snapped to attention. For the next few minutes, Barry watched them, narrow eyed. They went into ranks six deep. They wheeled, they turned about, they marched this way and that, and back again.

"Tortuga," Barry Watson snapped to the sergeant.

The non-com rasped.

Of a sudden, ranks closed tight. The first file lowered its shields, the second, crowded behind, extended their own over the heads of the first rank so that their drill shields topped the others. Behind, the third rank, and fourth held their shields above their heads, horizontally. The fifth and sixth ranks had about faced sharply and duplicated the shield wall. They were a living war tank.

Barry grunted unhappily, tugging at his right ear. He said to Stevens, "That's a Roman maneuver, actually. These cloddies aren't doing it any too well."

He turned to one of the drill sergeants. "That man at the end of the third file, sergeant."

"Yes, sir."

"Have him over here."

The sergeant barked commands.

Terry Stevens said, "What's the matter?"

"Is that recruit a new man or something?"

"No," Stevens said uncomfortably. "He's got family troubles. He's got a lot on his mind."

Barry looked at him. "Haven't we all? Who told him he had a mind? He's a phalanx man."

The cohort had ground to a halt again. In a moment, the footman in question approached at the double. He faced the two Earthmen and came to a half-hearted salute. His lack of enthusiasm wasn't lost on Barry Watson.

Watson looked at him for a long moment. "You don't seem to have your heart in this, spearman."

The other said nothing.

The Earthman said, "The whole theory is that every man moves exactly so. Just one man doesn't and the whole thing falls apart. In combat, that's a matter of life and death. Let those nomad funkers break your ranks, and you've all had it. You should know all this. Answer me!"

The footman said, his voice surly, "I should be working in the fields. This is not the season for war. It is the season to plant and hoe. It is not fitting that the strongest should be playing at war, with spears without points and shields made of cloth, while the women and children are in the fields."

"I see," Barry Watson said, his voice very level. "Then let me tell you this, spearman. You are not needed in the fields with your hoe. Specialist MacBride has succeeded in exploiting the islands off the coast. Technician Hawkins has introduced your people to the plow and reaper. The women and the new war prisoners are capable of producing more in the fields than was ever done before when you were breaking your back with your hoe. You *are* needed to defend the State against the nomads and rebels."

"The nomads were no danger until..." the footman began, his voice low still.

Barry Watson turned to the sergeant. "Flog this man," he snapped. "If he is able to move in less than a week, you answer for it."

"Yes, sir!"

Barry looked at another of the non-coms. The man's face was stolid and empty. They were good men, drawn from the ranks of the Khan's standing bodyguard. They were warriors born, and Barry Watson knew they were heart and soul behind the innovations he was making. Nothing succeeds like success, he knew, and these professionals knew success when they saw it. So far as the drill sergeants were concerned, there was no resentment against this instructor from space.

The Earthman snapped: "Take over the drill, sergeant. These men are going to be ready for the field by the end of the week. Understand?"

"Yes, sir."

Barry looked at his companion. "Walk on over here with me, Terry. I have something."

They strolled toward the side of the drill field, Stevens scowling un-happily.

"You sure that was a good idea?"

"What? Having that man flogged?"

Stevens said nothing for a moment, then, finally, "There's only eight of us—and Isobel."

Barry Watson grunted sour humor. "And that's probably the reason I should have had him shot for insubordination, instead of simply whipped. Tula is at war. Joe Chessman has the right idea. You don't run a military machine by being humanitarian, Terry."

"Maybe there was some other way to do it," Stevens muttered.

"Some other way of uniting Texcoco?" Barry grinned at him. "You should have come up with it sooner, friend. It would've saved me a lot of grief."

Stevens took a deep breath. "What'd you want to talk about, Barry?"

The other stopped and turned. He said evenly, "Mynor has defected. The Chief Priest. He's gone over to the nomads and rebels."

Stevens pursed his lips and thought about it. "He's a big wig on this planet. That religion of his is pretty well worldwide. What does Leonid Plekhanov think it will mean?"

Watson said sourly, "He's dithering, as usual. Joe was in favor of rounding up Mynor's closest associates and shooting them before they have a chance to take off too."

"Holy Jumping Zen," Stevens protested. "Plekhanov stopped that idea, didn't he?"

"Yes. As predictable. Our intrepid leader is great with his books, or in debate with somebody like Amschel Mayer, but when it comes to think-ing on his feet, he dithers."

"Well, I'd rather have Plekhanov dithering, than Joe Chessman running around shooting everybody that doesn't look right to him."

Barry Watson said thoughtfully, "I don't know, Terry. I don't know. Sometimes by shooting one or two, you don't have to shoot one or two thousand a few weeks later."

Terry Stevens said, "And by shooting one or two thousand, you don't have to shoot ten or twenty thousand a month later?"

Watson laughed, though without humor. "You're beginning to get it." But then he sobered. "I didn't ask for this job, Terry. But if this planet is ever going to become united, we've got to have a military to do it. It's an-archy now. Mynor and his rebels want only one thing: to turn the wheels backward to the old days."

"It's their world," Stevens muttered.

Barry Watson laughed his humorless laugh again. "Whose side are you on? Remember us? We're the handful of specialists sent out by the Office of Galactic Colonization to bring this world into the human community. Nobody thought it was going to be fun."

"I suppose so," Stevens said. "I'm just tired."

Watson grinned. "You'll be more tired tomorrow. I'm leaving you and Steve Cogswell in charge when we go up to the *Pedagogue* to confer with Amschel Mayer and his team. Plekhanov is leaving Isobel, Dick Hawkins, MacBride and you and Cogswell to hold the fort."

"Shouldn't either he or Chessman be here?"

Barry winked. "He's afraid to leave Joe Chessman. He labors under the illusion that Joe is his only rival for Hot Pants Sanchez."

Stevens flushed.

Barry Watson cocked his head and looked at his colleague narrowly. "Don't tell me our good doctor has got to you, too. Why don't you take a lesson from Cogswell and round yourself up a bevy from the Tulan curves? With the man shortage that's beginning to develop around here, we're developing the largest number of round heeled mopsies known in history."

"You think it's a good example for us to be setting?" Stevens said accusingly.

Watson shrugged as he turned to make off. "I'll be a cloddy if I know. I suppose we have to keep the birthrate up somehow."

* * * *

Leonid Plekhanov returned to the *Pedagogue* with a certain ostentatious ceremony. He was accompanied by Joe Chessman, Natt Roberts and Barry Watson of his original group, but four young, hard-eyed, hard-faced and armed Tulans were also in the party.

Their space lighter swooped in, nestled to the *Pedagogue*'s hull in the original bed it had occupied on the trip from Terra City, and her port opened to the corridors of the mother ship.

Plekhanov, flanked by Chessman and Watson, strode heavily toward the ship's lounge. Natt Roberts and two of the Tulans remained with the small boat and busied themselves acquiring various items they wished to take back to Texcoco on the return.

The two other natives followed the Earthmen to the lounge, their eyes going here and there in continued amazement, in spite of their efforts to appear untouched by it all. They were in full uniform, in the leather jerkins and kilts that had been adopted by Chessman for his troops. At their sides were short swords. In this they differed from their Earthling officers all of whom wore pistols.

Amschel Mayer was already seated at the officers' table. His face displayed his irritation at the other's methods of presenting himself. "Good Heavens, Plekhanov, what is this, an invasion?"

The other registered surprise.

Mayer indicated the Texcocans. "Do you think it necessary to bring armed men aboard the *Pedagogue*? Frankly, I have not even revealed to a single Genoese the existence of the ship."

Jerry Kennedy was seated to one side of Mayer, Natalie Wieliczka to the other. They were the only members of the Genoa team who had accompanied him for this meeting. Kennedy winked at Watson and Chessman and Watson grinned back but held his peace. He was trying to think of some manner in which to get Natalie aside, and for the moment, couldn't.

Plekhanov sank into a chair, rumbling, "We hold no secrets from the Texcocans. The sooner they advance to where they can utilize our libraries and laboratories, the better. And the fact that these boys are armed has no significance. My Tulans are currently embarked on a campaign to unite the planet. Arms are sometimes necessary, and Tula, my capital, is somewhat of an armed camp. All able-bodied men—"

Mayer broke in heatedly. "And this is the method you use to bring civilization to Texcoco? Is this what you consider the purpose of the Office of Galactic Colonization? An armed camp! How many persons have you slaughtered thus far?"

Joe Chessman sent a dour look at the two Tulans who were standing in the background. He looked back at Mayer. "Easy," he said.

Amschel Mayer spun on him. "I need no instruction from you, Chessman. Please remember I am senior in charge of this expedition and as such rank you."

Plekhanov thudded a heavy hand on the table. "I'll call my assistants to order, Mayer, if I feel it necessary. Admittedly, when this expedition left Terra City you were the ranking officer. Now, however, we're divided—at your suggestion, please remember. Now there are two independent groups and you no longer have jurisdiction over mine. You can hardly expect to supervise developments on Texcoco by getting together with us once every ten years. We'll go our own way, Mayer."

"Indeed!" Mayer barked. "And suppose I decide to withhold the use of the *Pedagogue*'s libraries and laboratories to you. I tell you, Plekhanov —"

Leonid Plekhanov interrupted him coldly. "I would not suggest you attempt any such step, Mayer. For one thing, I doubt if you have the... ability to carry it out."

Natalie Wieliczka was looking from one to the other of them in dismay. "Gentlemen, gentlemen," she said gently. "We're all colleagues."

Barry Watson chuckled. "Second the motion," he said. "What's all this jetsam about, anyway?"

Mayer glared but suddenly reversed himself. "Let's settle down and become more sensible. This is the first conference of the five we have scheduled. Ten years have elapsed. Actually, of course, we'd had some idea of each other's progress since team members sometimes meet on trips back here to the *Pedagogue* to consult the library, or do some work in one of the laboratories or shops. I am afraid, my dear Leonid, that your theories on rapid industrialization are being proven inaccurate."

"Nonsense!" Plekhanov rumbled in complete disgust. "The opposite is true."

Mayer said smoothly, "In the decade past, my team's efforts have more than tripled the Genoese industrial potential. Last week, one of our steamships crossed the second ocean. We've located petroleum and the first wells are going down. We've introduced a dozen crops that had disappeared through misadventure to the original colonists, including maize and oats. And, oh yes, our first railroad is scheduled to begin running between Bari and Ronda next spring. There are six new universities, including three Doctor Wieliczka has established to concentrate on medicine, and in the next decade I expect twenty more."

"Very good, indeed," Plekhanov grumbled.

"Only a beginning," Mayer pursued. "The breath of competition, of enterprise is sweeping Genoa. Feudalism crumbles. Customs, mores and traditions that have held up progress for a century or more are now on their way out."

Joe Chessman growled. "Some of the boys tell me you've had a few difficulties with this crumbling feudalism thing. In fact, didn't Buchwald barely escape with his life when the barons on your southern continent united to suppress all chartered cities?"

Mayer's thin face had darkened. "Never fear, my dear Joseph, those barons responsible for shedding the blood of southern hemisphere elements of progress will shortly pay for their crimes."

"You've got military problems, too, then?" Barry Watson asked him. "It seemed to me you were suggesting that only we on Texcoco have had to resort to strong arm tactics." There was an amused element in the younger man's voice.

Mayer's eyes went to him in irritation. "Some of the free cities of Genoa are planning measures to regain their property and rights on the southern hemisphere. This has nothing to do with my team, except, of course, in so far as we might sell them supplies or equipment."

The lanky Watson laughed lowly. "You mean like selling them a few quick firing breech loaders and trench mortars?"

Plekhanov muttered, "That will be enough, Barry."

But Mayer's eyes had widened. "How did you know about that?" He whirled on Plekhanov. "You're spying on me, trying to negate my work!"

Plekhanov rumbled, "Don't be a fool, Mayer. My team has neither the time nor interest to spy on you. We have our own work to do."

"Then how did you know—"

Barry Watson said mildly, "I was doing some investigating in the ship's library. I ran into evidence that you people had already used the blueprints for breech loaders and trench mortars." He shrugged. "I wasn't particularly interested."

Jerry Kennedy came to his feet and strolled over to the messroom bar. He said, "This seems to be an all-out spat rather than a conference to compare progress. Let's try to clear the air a bit. Anybody for a drink? Natalie, you used to like dry sherry, didn't you."

"Good heavens," Natalie Wieliczka said. "Is there still sherry there? I'd quite forgotten about sherry."

Kennedy said, "Frankly, that's the next thing I'm going to introduce to Genoa—some halfway decent guzzle. Do you know what those benighted heathens drink now? They ferment a berry and wind up with a sweetish wine that tastes something like blackberry cordial and runs about eight percent alcohol."

Watson grinned. "Make mine whiskey, Jerry. You've got no complaints. Our benighted heathens have a national beverage fermented from a plant similar to cactus. Ought to be drummed out of the human race."

Barry Watson had spoken idly, as had Kennedy, both forgetful of the two Tulan guards who were stationed at the doorway. One of the natives flushed slightly, but the other's resentment was only deep in his eyes.

Kennedy passed drinks around for everyone except the two Tulan soldiers and Amschel Mayer who shook his head in distaste. If only for a brief spell, some of the tenseness left the air while the men from Earth sipped their beverages.

Jerry Kennedy looked down into the glass into which he had poured a hefty shot of cognac. "Mother's milk," he muttered. He looked across the table. "Well, you've heard our report. How go things on Texcoco?"

"According to plan," Plekhanov rumbled. He threw his double vodka down.

Mayer snorted disbelief.

Plekhanov said ungraciously, "Our prime effort is now the uniting of the total population into one strong whole—a super-state capable of accomplishing the goals set us by the Co-ordinator. Everything else we do is secondary to forming such a state."

Mayer sneered. "Undoubtedly this goal of yours, this super-state, is being established by force. Nothing else could do it."

"Not always," Joe Chessman said. "Quite a few of the tribes join up on their own. Why not? The State has a great deal to offer them."

"Such as what?" Kennedy said mildly. He swirled his cognac in the large glass, smelled the bouquet and sighed.

Chessman looked at him in irritation. "Such as advanced medicine, security from famine, military protection from more powerful nations. The opportunity for youth to get an education and find advancement in the State's government, if they've got it on the ball."

"And what if they don't have it on the ball?"

Chessman growled. "What happens to such under any society? They get the dirty-end-of-the-stick jobs." His eyes went from Kennedy to Mayer, and there was contempt in his expression. "Are you suggesting that you offer anything better on Genoa?"

Mayer said, "Already on most of Genoa it is a matter of free competition. The person with ability is able to profit by it."

Joe Chessman grunted sour amusement. "Of course, it doesn't help to be the son of a wealthy merchant or a big politician—or, better still, a member of the *Pedagogue*'s complement."

Plekhanov took over. "In any society the natural leaders come to the top in much the same manner as the big ones come to the top in a bin of potatoes; they just work their way up."

Jerry Kennedy had finished with savoring the aroma of his cognac. He threw the drink back, then said easily, "At least those at the top can claim they're the biggest potatoes. They've been doing it down through the ages. Remember back in the twentieth century when Hitler and his gang announced they were the big potatoes in Germany and men of Einstein's stature fled the country—being small potatoes, I suppose."

Amschel Mayer said impatiently, "We continue to get away from the subject. Pray go on, my dear Leonid. You say you are forcibly uniting all Texcoco, requiring all to join this super-state of yours."

"We are uniting all Texcoco," Plekhanov corrected with a scowl at the other's prodding. "Not always by force. And that is by no means our only effort. We are weeding out the most intelligent of the assimilated peoples and educating them as rapidly as possible. We've introduced iron..."

"And use it chiefly for weapons," Natalie said lowly. She had been looking at Barry Watson, as though wondering at the changes ten years had wrought in him.

Plekhanov switched his scowl to her. "We've also introduced antibiotics, Doctor Wieliczka, and other medicines. And a field agriculture." He looked back to Kennedy. "We're rapidly building roads..."

"Military roads," Kennedy mused, looking down into his empty glass.

"...to all sections of the State. We've made a beginning in naval science and, of course, haven't ignored the arts."

"On the face of it," Mayer nodded, "hardly approaching what we have accomplished on Genoa."

Plekhanov rumbled indignantly. "We started two ethnic periods behind you. Even the Tulans, our most advanced people, were still using bronze, but your Genoese had iron and even gunpowder. Our advance is a bit slow to get moving Mayer, but when it begins to roll—"

Mayer gave his characteristic snort. "A free people need never worry about being passed by a subjected one."

Barry Watson came to his feet and made his way over to the bar. He picked up a bottle of whiskey that Kennedy had opened earlier, and poured himself another slug. He looked back over his shoulder at Amschel Mayer. "It's interesting the way you throw about that term *free*. Just what type of government do you sponsor?"

Mayer snapped. "Our team does not interfere in governmental forms, Watson. The various nations are free to adapt to whatever local conditions decree. They range from some under feudalistic domination to countries with varying degrees of republican democracy. Our base of operations in the eastern hemisphere is probably the most advanced of all the chartered cities on Genoa. It amounts to a city-state somewhat similar to Florence during the Renaissance."

"And your team finds itself in the position of the Medici, I assume."

"You might use that analogy. The Medici might have been, well, tyrants of Florence, dominating her finances and trade as well as her political government, but they were benevolent tyrants."

"Yeah," Watson grinned. "The thing about a benevolent tyranny, though, is that it's up to the tyrants to decide what's benevolent. I'm not so sure there's a great basic difference between your governing of Genoa and ours of Texcoco."

"Don't be a yoke," Mayer snapped. "We are granting the Genoese political freedoms as fast as they can assimilate them."

Joe Chessman growled, "But I imagine it's surprising to find how slowly they can assimilate. A moment ago you said they were free to form any government they wished. Now you say you feed them what you call freedom, only so fast as they can assimilate it."

"Obviously, we encourage them along whatever path we think will most quickly develop their economy," Mayer argued. "That's what we've been sent here to do. We stimulate competition, encourage all progress, political as well as economic."

Plekhanov lumbered to his feet and joined Kennedy at the bar. He growled at the other team head. "Amschel, obviously we are getting nowhere with this conference. I propose we adjourn to meet again at the end of the second decade."

Kennedy poured the other another shot of vodka, and filled his own glass again.

Amschel Mayer said, "I suppose it would be futile to suggest you give up this impossible totalitarian scheme of yours and reunite the expedition."

Plekhanov merely grunted his disgust.

Barry Watson said, "You might remember that it was your idea in the first place. It's too late to change now."

Jerry Kennedy said, "One thing." He frowned and swirled his cognac in the big glass. "What stand have you taken on giving your planet immortality?"

No one noticed the two Tulan men at arms shoot startled looks at each other.

"Immortality?" Chessman grunted. "We haven't got it to give."

"You know what I mean. It wouldn't take long to extend the life span double or triple the present," Jerry Kennedy said.

Amschel Mayer pursed his thin lips. "At this stage progress is faster with the generations closer together. A man is pressed when he knows he has only twenty or thirty years of peak efficiency. We on Earth are inclined to settle back and take life as it comes. For instance, you younger men are all past the century mark, but none have bothered to get married as yet."

Barry Watson shot a look at Natalie, who flushed slightly. "Plenty of time for that," he grinned.

"That's what I mean," Mayer said. "But a Texcocan or Genoese feels pressed to wed in his twenties, or earlier, to get his family under way."

"There's another element," Plekhanov muttered. He tossed his straight drink back, stiff wristed. "The more the natives progress, the more nearly they will equal our abilities. I wouldn't want anything to happen to our overall plans. As it is now, their abilities taper off at sixty and they reach senility at seventy or eighty. I think until the end we should keep it this way."

"A cold blooded view," Kennedy said. "If we extend their life expectancy, their best men would live to be of additional use to planet development."

"But they would not have our dreams," Plekhanov rumbled. "Such men might try to subvert us, and, just possibly, might succeed."

"I think Leonid is right," Mayer admitted with reluctance.

* * * *

It was obvious that the discussion was going to continue for at least a time. Barry Watson got Natalie Wieliczka's eye and made a motion toward the ship's library with his head. She looked about the others, then nodded very slightly. Barry drifted, unnoticed, from the lounge and waited for her behind some of the tape racks. She wasn't long in coming.

He put his hands on her shoulders. "It's been a long time, Polack," he told her softly. "Ten years."

Natalie looked up into his face. "Yes."

He let his arms go down and around her. "I've come up here, oh a dozen times on research. Thought maybe I'd run into you."

"I've spent quite a bit of time here in the library," she said lowly. "We just didn't coincide."

He kissed her. For a moment, a briefest of moments, her lips were tense. Then they relaxed.

She said, "Oh, Barry. So long a time. So long."

He held her away from him for a moment and looked into her face. "You haven't changed your mind?"

She shook her head, mute.

He said, "Like you say, ten years is forever. You sure you haven't found yourself a... a Genoese, to... to pass the hours?"

She shook her head.

There was a teasing element in his voice now. "Or Jerry Kennedy, or Mike Dean, one of our own group?"

She shook her head still once again and took a deep breath. "No. Nobody, Barry."

He kissed her and let his right hand drift lower down her back. He pressed her closer. She stiffened slightly but didn't resist.

Barry Watson looked at her questioningly. "You're tired, Natalie."

She gave a little snort of deprecation. "Isn't Isobel Sanchez? What does an M.D. do when she is the sole competent doctor on a whole planet? One doctor, one billion patients."

He laughed lowly. "What *do* you do? I have a sneaking suspicion not exactly what Isobel has come up with."

She said, "Why, I've established three medical universities, one on each continent. I'm trying to teach teachers. I get one going and move on to the third. Then back to the first." She paused and took a deep breath as though in frustration.

"And?"

"And by the time I've made the complete circuit, they've got back to powdering frogs for medicine, murmuring incantations and spells, and bleeding their patients. I have to start all over." She shook her head. "Perhaps I'm using the wrong method. I wish Isobel Sanchez had come up. I'd like to confer with her. What is she doing? What *can* you do when you are one and you have a billion patients?"

He grinned at her. "You can let nine hundred million, nine hundred thousand of them go to pot and work on what's left."

She frowned at him.

He said, a shade of impatience at the trend of talk in his voice, "Isobel isn't bothering with anybody except our Tulans. She's had them build a swanky hospital. She's training a handful of them, or, rather, letting them train themselves." He chuckled sourly. "She has a knack for picking the best looking physical specimens to become her male nurses cum interns. Old Leonid must be blind. At any rate, she's introduced antibiotics and so forth. Actually, her glamour boys learn fast. She's letting them get into the *Pedagogue*'s tapes as fast as they can assimilate them."

Natalie said thoughtfully, "I've got to get more basic medical books into print."

He kissed her again. "Zen take this fling, Polack. Let those cloddies in the lounge talk shop. How about us?"

"How do you mean, Barry?"

"Just that. It's been ten years, Polack. Are we going to let it be another ten?"

She frowned at him, lacking understanding. "But you're on Texcoco and I'm on Genoa, Barry. What can we do?"

He was impatient. "Look, let's not be a couple of flats. You have access to your team's space lighter, I have access to ours. Fine. Let's make a date. I'll tell old Plekhanov I've got to check up on the differences between the Theban and Macedonian phalanxes, and why it was the Romans were able to take the Macedonians a couple of hundred years after Alexander. Meanwhile, you can tell Amschel that there's a new epidemic or something, and you have to come up here for a few day's study."

"A few days?"

"Sure. We'll have a real party. There's still lots of Earthside liquor on board and..."

She was shaking her head, hard. "No. Oh, no, Barry. That's not what we want!"

He scowled at her. "Ten years is a long time, Natalie. I'm a man, not a robot. It's what *I* want. Do you love me or not?"

She turned from him abruptly and ran back toward the lounge.

"Hey!" he called. "Don't be drivel happy."

Natt Roberts entered the library. He looked back over his shoulder at the retreating Natalie. "What's the matter?" he said.

Barry Watson swore under his breath. "Nothing," he said.

Roberts shrugged. "The team's getting ready to leave," he said. "Plekhanov wants to know where you are."

"I'm coming," Watson snarled.

* * * *

Later, in the space lighter heading back for Genoa, Amschel Mayer said speculatively, "Did you notice anything about Leonid Plekhanov?"

Jerry Kennedy was piloting. He said, "He seems the same irascible old bird he's always been."

Natalie's mind was on other things. "A bit tired," she said. "But we're all that. Both teams."

But the group leader wasn't to be put off. "It seems to me he's become a touch power mad. Could the pressures he's under cause his mind to slip? Obviously, all isn't peaches and cream in that attempt of his to achieve world government on Texcoco."

"Well," Kennedy muttered, "all isn't peaches and cream with us, either. The barons are far from licked, especially in the west." He changed the subject. "By the way, that banking deal went through in Pola. I was able to get control."

"Fine," Mayer chuckled. "You must be quite the richest man in the city. There is a certain stimulation in this financial game, Jerry, isn't there?"

"Uh huh," Jerry told him. "Of course, it doesn't hurt to have a marked deck."

"Marked deck?" Natalie said, frowning.

"That's right. It's handy that gold is the medium of exchange on Genoa," Jerry said. "Especially in view of the fact that we have a machine on the ship capable of changing metals."

CHAPTER VI

LEONID PLEKHANOV, Joseph Chessman, Barry Watson, Khan Reif and several of the Tulan army staff stood on a knoll overlooking a valley of several square miles. A valley dominated on all sides but the sea by steep mountain ranges.

Reif and the three Earthlings were bent over a folding table which held a large military map of the area. Barry Watson traced with his finger.

"There are only two major passes into this valley. We have this one; they dominate that." He turned and pointed at the sea. "We can anchor our left flank on the sea. The heavy cavalry, armed with the muskets. They'll have no trouble holding there. If the action gets hot enough, they can even wade out into the surf." He went back to the map and traced again with his finger, thinking it out as he went.

"The phalanx will extend here, about a mile or so. Across the flat plain. The terrain is ideal. At the right flank, light cavalry and auxiliary troops. They're our weakest element, but they can skirmish up into these hills indefinitely. The terrain is such that the enemy will have a hard time utilizing his cavalry."

Leonid Plekhanov was scowling, out of his element and knowing it. "How many men has Mynor been able to get together?"

Barry Watson avoided looking into the older man's face. "Approximately half a million, according to Dick Hawkins' estimate. He flew over them this morning." Barry jabbed at the map again. "They're coming down here, by these two roads. Their line of march extends..."

"Half a million!" Plekhanov blurted. There was almost an element of accusation in his voice.

Barry said, "Including the nomads, of course."

Joe Chessman growled. "The nomads fight more like a mob than an army."

Plekhanov was shaking his massive head. "Most of them will melt away if we continue to avoid battle as we have been doing. They can't feed that many men on the countryside. The nomads, in particular, will return home if they don't get a fight soon."

Watson hid his impatience. "That's the point, sir. If we don't break their power now, in a decisive defeat, we'll have them to fight again, later.

And already they've got iron swords, the crossbow and even a few muskets. Given time and they'll all be so armed. Then the fat'll be in the fire. There's another element, too. Our strength is in our infantry; they dominate the countryside with their cavalry. The cities and towns that have come over to us are hard to protect with, our limited number of men. They're wavering in their loyalty. We've got to be able to protect them."

"He's right," Chessman said sourly.

The Khan, Reif, nodded his head as did his general officers. "We must finish them now," he said. "If we can. The task will be twice as great next year."

Plekhanov grumbled in irritation. "Half a million of them, and something like forty thousand of our Tulans, most of them armed with nothing more than overgrown spears. Why, they could trample that number of men to death."

Reif corrected him. "Some thirty thousand Tulans, all infantrymen." He added, "And eight thousand allied cavalry, only some of whom can be trusted." Reif's ten year old son came up next to him and peered down at the map.

"What's that child doing here?" Plekhanov snapped in continued irritation.

The boy looked up at him calmly, then at his father. There was a strength in the lad's face, strength and calm, duplicating his father.

Reif looked into the Earthling's face. "This is Taller Second, my son. You from First Earth have never bothered to study our customs. One of them is that a Khan's son participates in all battles his father does. It is his training. One day, without doubt, he will lead the armies of the People."

Plekhanov snorted ungraciously.

Barry Watson had turned back to the map, and was demonstrating again, his finger touching here, there. "They are coming down through here as fast as they can. They probably figure that at last they've got us at bay. They're moving fast, and tiring themselves and their horses. By the time they get here, we'll have had lots of rest, lots of time for preparation. It will take a full three days for their whole army to get through this defile." He touched it with his finger. "It's narrow." He added with emphasis. "In retreat, it would take them the same time to get out."

Plekhanov said heavily, "We can't risk it. If we were defeated, we have no reserve army. We'd have lost everything." He looked at Joe Chessman and Watson significantly. "We'd have to flee back to the *Pedagogue*."

Reif's face was expressionless, but his eyes went from one of the Earthlings to the other.

Barry Watson looked at him. "We won't desert you, Reif, forget about that aspect of it. We're all of us in this together."

Reif said, "I believe you, Barry Watson. You are a... soldier."

Dick Hawkins' small biplane zoomed in, landed expertly at the knoll's foot. It was a simple craft, propeller driven, and with a light machine gun mounted to fire directly ahead. A one seater scout, its pay load consisted of pilot and a few bombs. The occupant vaulted out and approached them at a half run.

His arrival coincided with that of Isobel Sanchez, who came up mounted on a snow white horse, richly saddled. She looked as though she was on a pleasure ride and came accompanied by two maids and a trio of her young, handsome interns.

Hawkins called out as soon as he was within shouting distance. "They're moving in. Their advance cavalry units are already in the pass. The main body is only a day's march behind."

When he was with them, Plekhanov rubbed his hand nervously over heavy lips. He rumbled, "Their cavalry, eh? Well, let's teach them a lesson. Listen, Hawkins, get back there and dust them. Use the gas. That'll slow them up. Terrify the horses."

The pilot said slowly, "I have four bullet holes in my wings."

"Bullet holes?" Isobel said. She was slightly miffed by the lack of attention her arrival had precipitated. She had dismounted and moved to Leonid Plekhanov's side, taking him by one heavy arm. "I thought it was only our side that had guns. Zen, this whole thing begins to get dangerous."

They ignored her.

"Bullet holes?" Joe Chessman repeated.

Dick Hawkins turned to him. "By the looks of things, MacBride's whole unit has gone over to the rebels. Complete with their double barreled muskets. A full thousand of them."

Chessman closed his eyes, wearily. "How about MacBride?"

"I don't know, Joe. All I saw was his cavalry fraternizing with the lead elements of Mynor's force."

Watson looked frigidly at Leonid Plekhanov. "You insisted on issuing those guns to men that we weren't really sure of, then putting them under command of a man without military background. Why didn't you let one of Reif's officers head that detachment, somebody that would have recognized trouble when it started?"

Plekhanov grumbled, "Confound it, don't use that tone of voice with me. We have to arm our men, don't we? And as far as MacBride is concerned, I like to keep command in the hands of our group."

Watson said, "Our still comparatively few advanced weapons shouldn't go into the hands of anybody but trusted citizens of the State, certainly not to a bunch of mercenaries. If you can buy a mercenary, so can your enemy. He can buy him right from under you with more money. The only ones we can really trust, even among the Tulans—excuse me Reif, obviously I don't mean you and your officers—are those that were kids when we first took over. The ones we've had time to indoctrinate."

"The mistake's made. It's too late now," Plekhanov said doggedly. "Hawkins, go on back and dust those cavalrymen as they come through the pass. Maybe we can throw enough of a scare into them that they'll retreat."

The seldom speaking Khan said now, "It was a mistake, too, to allow them the secret of the crossbow. It is a weapon almost as dangerous as the musket."

Plekhanov suddenly angry beyond the bounds of his ragged temper, roared, "I didn't *allow* them anything. Once the crossbow was introduced to our own people, it was simply a matter of time before its method of construction got to the enemy."

There was the faintest of frowns on the forehead of Isobel Sanchez, she looked from Plekhanov to Reif, and squeezed tighter the pudgy arm of her lover as though to regain confidence.

Reif's eyes were unflinching from the Earthman's. He said, "Then the crossbow should never have been introduced. It wasn't necessary for the military plans Barry Watson has made for us."

Plekhanov ignored him. He said, "Hawkins, get going on that dusting. Maybe you can scare them away. Watson, pull what units we already have in this valley back through the pass we control. We'll avoid battle until more of their army has fallen away."

Hawkins said with deceptive mildness, "I just told you those cavalrymen have muskets. To fly low enough to use the gas on them, I'd have to get within easy range. That pass is narrow. Point one, this is the only aircraft we have, and it's priceless for reconnaissance. Point two, one of our number, MacBride is already dead as a result of poor decisions. Point three, I came on this expedition to help modernize the Texcocans, not to die in battle."

Plekhanov snarled at him. "Coward, eh? Alright, we'll turn the aircraft over to Roberts, or somebody else who can take commands." He turned churlishly to Watson and Reif. "Start pulling back our units. We can be completely out of this valley before Mynor can get his full force here."

Barry Watson took a deep breath and looked at Joe Chessman. "Joe?"

Isobel Sanchez dropped the arm of Plekhanov she had been holding. A tiny tongue tip protruded from her overly red lips, and her eyes darted from one of the men to the other.

Joe Chessman shook his head slowly. He said to Reif, "Khan, start bringing your infantrymen through the pass. Barry, we'll follow your plan of battle. We'll anchor one flank on the sea and concentrate what cavalry we can trust on the hills to the right. You're correct, that's going to be the crucial spot. That right flank has to hold while the phalanx does its job."

Plekhanov's thick lips trembled. He said in fury, "Is this insubordination?"

Reif looked from Plekhanov to Chessman, then turned and followed by young Taller and two of his staff, started down the hill to where their horses were tethered.

Chessman turned to Dick Hawkins. "If you've got the fuel, Dick, maybe it would be a good idea to keep them under observation. Fly high enough, of course, to avoid any gunfire."

Hawkins darted a look at the infuriated Plekhanov, then turned and hurried back to his plane.

Joe Chessman, his voice sullen, said to Plekhanov, "We can't afford any more mistakes, Leonid. We've had too many already." He said to Watson, "Be sure and let their cavalry units scout us out. Allow them to see that we're entering the valley. They'll think they've got us trapped."

"They will have!" Plekhanov roared. "I counter that order, Watson! We're withdrawing."

Barry Watson raised his eyebrows at Joe Chessman.

"Put him under arrest," Joe growled sourly. "We'll have to decide what to do about it later."

Barry snapped an order to two of the remaining Tulans.

Isobel Sanchez came up to the stolid Chessman, her eyes shining. She said, "Joe, don't let it worry you. You did what you had to do. I'm proud of you."

He looked at her thoughtfully.

* * * *

By the third day, Mynor's rebel and nomad army had filed through the pass and was forming itself into battle array. Rank, upon rank, upon rank until the floor of the valley seemed carpeted with humanity and horses. Behind them slowly ground a seemingly endless wagon train pulled by oxen and mules.

The Tulan infantry had taken less than half a day to enter. They had camped and rested during the interval, the only action being on the part of the rival cavalry forces.

Now the thirty thousand Tulans went into their phalanx and began their slow march across the valley floor toward the enemy.

Joe Chessman, Hawkins, Natt Roberts and Khan Reif again occupied the knoll which commanded a full view of the terrain. With binoculars and wrist radios from the *Pedagogue* they kept in contact with the battle.

Below, Barry Watson walked behind the advancing infantry. He was armed only with a swagger stick, which he periodically tapped against his right knee.

There were six divisions of five thousand men each, twenty-four foot long *sarissas* stretched before their sixteen man deep line. Only the first few lines were able to extend their weapons; the rest gave weight and supplied replacements for the advancing lines' dead and wounded. Behind them all, the Tulan drums beat out the slow march.

Cogswell, beside Watson with his wrist radio, said excitedly, "Here comes a cavalry charge, Barry. Reif reports that right behind it the rebel infantry is coming in." Cogswell cleared his throat. "All of them."

Watson held up his hand in signal to his officers. The phalanx came to a halt, received the charge of nomad cavalry on the hedge of *sarissas*. The enemy horses wheeled and attempted to retreat to the flanks but were caught in a bloody confusion by the pressure of their own advancing infantry.

Watson muttered, "They thought they'd brush us aside with one wild attack."

Cogswell, his ear to the radio, said, "Their main body of horses is hitting our right flank." He wet his lips. "Terry Stevens is over there. He's outnumbered something like ten to one. At least ten to one."

"They've got to hold," Watson said. "Tell Reif and Chessman that flank has to hold, no matter what. You can't allow a phalanx to have a flank turned. It's too clumsy to maneuver. If those nomad funkers come around our end, we're sunk."

The enemy infantrymen in their hundreds of thousands hit the Tulan line in a clash of deafening military thunder. Barry Watson resumed his pacing. He signaled to the drummers, who beat out another march. The phalanx moved forward again slowly, and slowly went into their formation, each of the six divisions slightly ahead of the one following. Of necessity, the straight lines of the nomads and rebels had to break, and their line became a mob of raging warriors.

The Tulan drums went: *boom*, ah *boom*, ah *boom*, ah *boom*.

The Tulan phalanx moved slowly, obliquely across the valley. The hedge of spears ruthlessly pressed the mass of enemy infantry before them.

The sergeants paced behind, shouting over the din. "Dress it up, you bastards, you funkers. Dress it up! You spearman! Your spearpoint is three inches low. Dress it up!"

"You there," a sergeant yelled. "You've been hit. Fall out to the rear."

"I'm all right," the wounded spearman snarled, battle lust in his voice.

"Fall out, I said, you cloddy! Back to the dressing station. You there, take his place!"

The Tulan phalanx ground ahead.

One of the sergeants grinned wanly at Barry Watson as his men moved forward with the preciseness of the famed Rockettes of another era. "It's working," he said proudly. "All that drill. But it's working!"

Barry Watson snorted, and hit his leather kilt with his swagger stick. "Don't give me the credit," he said. "It belongs to another man a long ways away in both space and time."

Cogswell came up, worriedly. He reported: "Our right flank cavalry is falling back, being pushed up into the hills further. Joe Chessman wants to know if you can send any support."

Barry Watson's face went expressionless. "No," he said flatly. "It's got to hold. We need another hour. Possibly two. If the nomads get around that end, there won't be a Tulan alive by nightfall. Tell Joe and the Khan that flank can't be turned. Suggest they throw in those cavalry units they're not sure of. The ones that threatened mutiny last week."

"Dress it up, you funkers! Dress it up," the sergeants rasped. The phalanx ground forward, into the shouting, screaming mob opposed to them.

* * * *

Joe Chessman stood on the knoll flanked by the Khan's ranking officers and the balance of the Earthmen save Terry Stevens, who was somewhere in the cavalry fray. Natt Roberts was at the radio. He turned to the others and repeated Watson's message.

He added, "I can't raise Terry. Haven't been able to for the past fifteen minutes."

Joe Chessman looked out over the valley. The thirty thousand-man phalanx was pressing back the enemy infantry with the precision of a machine. He looked up the hillside to the point where the enemy cavalry was turning the right flank. Given cavalry behind the Tulan line and the battle was lost, as everyone involved realized.

"O.K., boys," Chessman growled sourly. "We're in the clutch now. All bets are down. Hawkins!"

"Yeah," the pilot said.

"See what you can do. Use what bombs you have, including the napalm. Fly as low as you can in the way of scaring their horses." He added, sourly, "Avoiding scaring ours, if you can."

"You're the boss," Hawkins said, and scurried off down the hill toward his scout plane.

Joe Chessman growled to the others. "When I was taking my degree in Primitive Society and Primitive Military Tactics, I didn't exactly have this in mind. Come on, boys!"

It was the right thing to say. The others laughed and took up their equipment, submachine guns, riot guns, a flame thrower, grenades, and followed him up the hill toward the fray.

Chessman said over his shoulder to Reif, "Khan, you're in the saddle. You can keep in touch with both us and Watson on the radio."

Reif hesitated only a moment. "There is no need for further direction of the battle from this point. A warrior is of more value now than a Khan. Come my son." He caught up a double barreled musket and followed the Earthmen and other Tulan officers. The ten year old Taller scurried after with a revolver.

Natt Roberts said, "If we can hold their cavalry for only another hour or so, Watson's phalanx will have their infantry pressed up against the pass they entered by. It took them three days to get through it; they're not going to be able to get out in a few hours."

"That's the idea," Joe Chessman said dourly. "Let's go."

* * * *

Terry Stevens and a lone Tulan sergeant, whose name he did not know, were making their stand in a shallow, natural depression in the shade of a raw cliff. The sergeant had taken earlier a crossbow arrow in his shoulder and under the circumstances they had been unable to dislodge it, the point being barbed. He had lost a lot of blood and his stolid face was pale.

Terry Stevens looked up at the cliff. He said, "Well, Joe said to hold the right flank. You can't get any further to the right than this. Not unless you're a bird."

The sergeant peered over the top of their improvised entrenchment. All up the slope were sprawled the bodies of Tulans and nomads, of cavalry horses and desertland ponies. There was a blast from below and a shattering against a nearby rock. The sergeant jerked his head down.

"You never hear the one that hits you," Terry Stevens told him.

"So I am told," the other growled. "But those muskets are double-barreled. Perhaps there is a second slug on the way."

Terry was looking out over the valley. "Barry Watson seems to be doing all right. See that tiny bug down there in the rear of the third division. I'll bet that's him."

The sergeant growled. "I wish I was in the rear of the third division."

Terry Stevens looked over at him worriedly, then took a quick peek over the embankment. He brought his submachine gun up quickly and let loose a short burst.

"Get him?" his companion said, disinterestedly.

"I don't know. I don't think so. They're slowly edging up. This time, they'll wait till they're close before they rush us."

The sergeant grunted sourly. "They don't know how many of us are here and they can't leave us, with these otherworld weapons in their rear." He switched subject. "Are you sure that talk-thing on your wrist won't work?"

Terry Stevens looked down at the shattered two-way radio on his wrist. He pulled it off and threw it aside. "Last word from Joe Chessman was to hold, no matter what. See the fighting down there? If this gang surrounding us was free to erupt around this flank, that'd be the end."

"It is the end for us, anyway," the sergeant said. "One more rush does it. There must be a thousand of them."

Stevens was peering over the embankment. He said, "Do you have any more of Cogswell's grenades?"

"No."

"There's a gang of them collecting in that arroyo down there."

The sergeant looked over at the body of one of his fallen cavalrymen. He squirmed toward the dead man, keeping head and body low. Their shelter was not overly deep. He ran his hands over the other's body, came up with a metal ball. He squirmed back to the Earthman, handed the small bomb over.

"Watch it with care," he growled. "It is one of the earlier models. You will blow your arm off if you do not watch it with care."

Terry Stevens hefted it, pulled the pin, lobbed it over the top of their shelter and pressed himself to the ground. There was a blast and they both raised their heads. Stevens shuddered.

The sergeant brought his weapon up and let fly another burst.

Stevens said, "Better watch the ammo."

The sergeant snorted dourly. "This is my last clip, but my arm stiffens. I will not be able to fire much longer."

Stevens looked at him anxiously. "Want some more of the pain killer?"

"No. It is not necessary. Already it is as though I float. It does not hurt, it is only that the arm stiffens." He peered over the rim of the crater-like depression. "They fight all the way from here to the valley floor. You can not tell our people from the natives. Do you realize we started with five hundred men? All dead, or will be when they root us out of here."

Stevens said mildly, "Some of the boys that were with us are still fighting down below."

The sergeant growled, "Well, it *looks* as though all five hundred are sprawled around here."

"How you and I survived is a mystery," Stevens muttered.

"It will not be for long. I wonder if there is more ammunition on any of those bodies close enough to get to."

"No. I shook them all down. I've got one extra clip here."

"That will not last long."

Terry said, "Look. Down there. A new group coming up. Look, there's Dick Hawkins in that little crate of his. He's flying air cover for them. It must be Joe Chessman and the rest. They'll all have automatic..."

A crossbow quarrel whirred above his head, missing him by millimeters. He ducked and shook his head ruefully. "I didn't even see where that one came from."

"How far are they?" the sergeant growled. He shifted his gun, trying to get it into a position so that he could rest it on the ground and fire with one arm.

"I don't know. A mile or two."

The sergeant grunted.

Terry Stevens fired another burst. "Here they come!" he rasped. He could hear the submachine gun of his companion blasting away beside him.

Up the hill scrambled a hundred or more black garbed nomads, shouting desert battle cries. Most of them carried viciously long, two-edged swords—long, thin lances. A small number were equipped with muskets.

"Get those fanatics out front!" Terry rasped. "Holy Men!" His gun burped, burped again. Fell silent. He slammed his hand against its side, dropping the empty clip. He fumbled at his belt, brought out the sole remaining ammunition he possessed. He jammed it into the gun, blasted again. Three of the ascending enemy toppled over, one to remain motionless, the other two screaming pain and fear.

Terry shot and shot again. "One curd of a place for a pacifist," he snarled.

It occurred to him that the other's gun had fallen silent. He darted a look at the sergeant, and then turned his face away quickly.

The charge was slowing as the dismounted enemy plowed up the steepness of the brief hill. Those who had fallen earlier hindered the way. Two got nearly to the summit only to fall over, shattered by a quick double burst from the automatic weapon of the defending Earthman.

And suddenly it was over for the nonce. The charge broke. The warriors turned and fled after the few with muskets had emptied them at the hilltop.

Terry Stevens, alone, tried to avoid looking at his companion. He ejected the clip from his gun, looked at it. He had exactly three rounds left. He reached over and took the sergeant's gun and checked the clip. It was empty.

He took a deep breath. "Okay, Joe," he muttered. "It's up to you now. The ultimate right flank is about to fold."

There was a roar above and he stared up, startled.

It was Dick Hawkins in his biplane. He waved over the edge of the open cockpit.

Terry Stevens waved back. "I wish the hell I was up there with you, you funker," he growled in sour humor. He could hear the musketmen blasting away at the aircraft. He waved his fellow Earthman away. "Get out of here, you cloddy! One of them will wing you with one of those blunderbusses," he yelled meaninglessly.

Hawkins was heading back toward the knot of men that were slowly shooting their way up the hillside, their magnified fire power, compared to that of the foe, clearing the way before.

Down in the valley, Barry Watson's men were still grinding forward. From Stevens' position, the whole field of action clearly visible, he could see the enemy forces beginning to pile up in the defile through which they had entered the valley during the week. Many of their horses were already in confusion, attempting retreat, but running into a mess of supply wagons, still attempting to enter by the narrow way.

Stevens grunted to himself. "Barry's made it. Trouble is, it's going to take the gang up here a long time to realize it." He poked his weapon over the side of the depression carefully. The nomads were going to be mustering for another rush soon. They must have noted, during the last one, how abruptly the fire had fallen off. They might even suspect that there was now but one man holding out here.

* * * *

Joe Chessman and Reif, blowing from the ascent, stared down into the crater where Stevens and the sergeant had held out for so long. Both men had been mutilated to the point of being unrecognizable.

Reif said, "He was not a warrior by choice. He fought well for one who was not a warrior."

Chessman looked at him. He looked back at the naked bodies and growled, "I suspect the campaign was won here. This was the ultimate crucial point."

Natt Roberts came slogging up, for once no longer the dandy. His uniform was soaked through with perspiration and his face was grimy and tired, blood and mud were on his usually natty boots. He had heard Chessman's words.

Roberts looked down at the body of his companion and muttered, "Now the question is, was it worth it?"

Chessman looked at him coldly.

CHAPTER VII

NATALIE WIELICZKA was saying, "We're going to have to have at least one sizeable hospital in each city of over a hundred thousand, and at least a clinic in the smaller towns."

Michael Dean looked at her wryly. He was seated at a heavy desk, littered with reports, graphs and receipts and was dressed in the colorful silks and furs of the highest class Genoese; he looked nothing so much as the middle years Henry the Eighth.

He grumbled, "Why come to me? I'm not the treasurer of this continent. Approach the governments involved. So you've got to the point where you need more hospitals. Fine, let them stick a new tax on the peasantry to finance them."

Natalie said patiently, though wearily, "You know better than that, Mike. Taxes are leveled on wealth, not poverty."

Mike Dean snorted. He was fond of Natalie Wieliczka, as everybody from the *Pedagogue* was fond of her, but of late she had been getting under his skin with her everlasting nagging for funds. He snorted. "Tell that to the peasants and the slums in town."

"That the poor don't pay taxes?" She raised her eyebrows. "They go through the motions, perhaps, but it's an optical illusion. The powers that be—such as yourself—would like the poor to think that taxes were a big issue they had to be concerned about. Get them all steamed up worrying about taxes, so that their real troubles will be ignored."

"You sound like a rabble rouser," Mike Dean chuckled.

But she went on, doggedly. "Suppose it's possible for a peasant or unskilled laborer, to get by on fifty crowns a day. Fine, you pay him one hundred crowns, and then tax him fifty. He *thinks* he's paying taxes and gets all in a dither about their magnitude, but in actuality if taxes went up another ten crowns a day, you boys in the saddle would have to raise his pay. If his cost of living fell off, the governments you keep in power would undoubtedly raise his taxes to that extent. On an average, he gets a living wage, just enough to get by on, no more, no less, so taxes don't really interest him."

Mike Dean said dryly, "Save me your economics, Natalie. The fact of the matter is, Lou and I are in no position to finance a project as big as you're talking about. We over-expanded, especially in textiles. Introducing the cotton gin was fine but things got steam rolling and before we knew it, we started producing cloth twice as fast as we can sell it. Everybody on this continent, who can afford a wardrobe, has a closet full of clothes."

Natalie said impatiently, "Introduce fashion."

"What?" He scowled at her.

She said, "I was joking, I suppose. But I'm surprised you haven't already. Between you and Amschel Mayer, you've introduced just about every other gimmick that..."

"Wait a minute," Dean said. "How do you mean, introduce fashion?"

"Fashion, fashion. Styles. So every woman on this continent has already got a closet full of clothes your textile products? Fine. Switch styles on them, drop the hemline five inches. Play it up in your publications. Have some of the big name theatrical people wear them. Introduce some fashion magazines. Make them feel as though they're underprivileged if they can't get a complete new wardrobe of the new styles."

Dean was staring at her. "Zen! I think you're right!"

Natalie muttered, "Forgive me, for I know not what I do."

"What?"

"Nothing," she said, coming to her feet. She looked down at him and far in the back of her eyes there was an element of contempt. "Mike, we came here to develop this world, not just to exploit it."

He looked up at her, defensively. "Sometimes it's hard to figure out where one starts and the other ends."

"In this particular case, it isn't. My medical universities are at last beginning to turn out competent practitioners. I need those hospitals, Mike."

"All right, all right, I'll talk it over with Louis. Listen, Natalie, how about you taking a week or so off and getting this fashion thing going for us? Neither Louis nor I know..."

She snorted in fine disgust. "Some chance, you miserable cloddy. I can just see myself. Already I feel like a traitor to my sex."

Mike Dean chuckled sourly. "Well, you can't blame me for trying."

A secretary entered. "The Honorable Rosetti."

Dean said, "Oh good. Show him in, Lange."

"At once, Honorable Dean." Lange left.

Natalie looked after the underling. "What's he cringing about?"

Dean shrugged. "It's an attitude you develop when you've got possibly three hundred crowns to your name."

She frowned at him. "I hope you don't encourage it. Wasn't the theory that on Genoa we were going to advance by utilizing man's freedoms? Plekhanov and Chessman are the advocates of the iron fist."

He shrugged again, uncomfortably. "You don't have to encourage it. It comes automatically." He stood as Louis Rosetti entered the room.

Rosetti, one of the older of the *Pedagogue*'s complement, smiled at Natalie. "Nice to see you, Doc. We don't get together often enough."

"Hello, Louis," she said wanly. "Not much time for social life."

Dean said, "It's not as nice as all that to see her. She's trying to shake us down for enough to pay off this city-state's national debt."

Rosetti looked at her. "Why don't you get after Mayer and Kennedy for a change? Didn't Mike tell you we were hurting?"

"It wouldn't be a change, Louis. I'm doing the same on their continent as I am here. If anything, my program is somewhat ahead over there."

Dean said, "What's up, Louis? I thought you were working on that series of distilleries."

"Distilleries!" Natalie said.

Mike Dean looked at her impatiently. "What's wrong with distilleries? It's not as though we're introducing alcohol. They've always had wine here."

She shook her head. "I suppose it's none of my affair. It seems to me, though, that we could first devote a few factories to medicinal products before getting around to stronger guzzle."

Louis Rosetti, who was dressed in much the same manner as his colleague, made a motion toward the next room with his head. "Presbyter Doul is out there."

"Who?"

"Doul, the Temple monk. He's taking a dim view of our production of rum and vodka."

"Is there a back way out of here?" Natalie said. "I'm having enough trouble with the Temple without tangling with any of them ranking as high as Presbyter."

Mike Dean led her to a rear door, then said to Rosetti with a sigh, "Show him in, Louis. We're going to have to play this carefully. Anybody as high in the hierarchy as this is not flat."

Louis Rosetti went back to the anteroom to return with a thin-faced, fox-like individual dressed in the dark robes of a Temple monk, but beneath them the rich garb of an upper-class Genoese of the highest income bracket.

Mike Dean went through the motions involved in a visit of such a dignitary, winding up with Presbyter Doul in the room's most comfortable chair.

The newcomer eyed him thoughtfully, as Dean returned to his desk, and Louis Rosetti found a seat of his own. The two Earthmen were wary.

Doul said, "You adapt quickly and well to our ways, my son."

Dean said carefully, "But your ways are our ways, Your Holiness."

The Temple hierarch said, "I wonder. It was first widely thought that you came from Bari, on the eastern continent, but upon inquiry to our associate Temple there, it seems as though on their part they were of the opinion that you and your equal numbers on the eastern continent had come from here."

"Our equal numbers?" Rosetti said cautiously.

The presbyter looked at him. "Yes, such as Honorable Mayer and his associates."

"Our connections with Amschel Mayer are on a business level," Dean said.

"So I understand. Very profitably so, but perhaps on other levels as well. Levels not quite clear to myself and my holy brothers of the Temple."

Dean shook his head, as though lacking understanding. He was on delicate ground now.

The other shrugged thin shoulders. "However, your origins are not of present concern." He paused. "Perhaps you are aware of the fact that my position involves the holy product of the vine, that I administer the holy production and distribution of this gift of the Supreme."

Louis Rosetti nodded. "We have been so informed, Your Holiness. In fact, if I understand correctly, your family has had this, ah, monopoly for at least a century. Your position is hereditary."

The Temple hierarch's eyes had narrowed again. "Do you see fit to criticize the method by which the Temple administers the holy gift of wine?"

Rosetti held up his hands, as though in horror. "Certainly not, Your Holiness."

"Very well. Then let this be understood. These new products you have introduced"—he made a face of disgust—"what are their names? Rum, vodka, gin, whiskey. All of them vile imitations of the holy product of the vine, gift of the Supreme to be used in sacred ceremony and only during selected holy days."

Mike Dean said, "But Your Holiness, these distilled products are not imitations of wine, they are new, ah, discoveries. Wine is, admittedly, the monopoly of the Temple. We would not dream of, ah, attempting to intrude on your, ah, income in this field. But our distilled products, which, as you know, have been received with enthusiasm..."

The presbyter cut him off by banging his fist against the arm of his chair. "Enthusiasm indeed! These vile brews are consumed night and day, every day, by all who can afford them! My secretaries estimate that literally millions are flowing into your coffers."

Dean tried to placate him. "Your Holiness, it is true that in the past the peasants and unskilled workers were issued wine only on special religious holidays. But the aristocracy and the other better-to-do elements of society, including Temple personnel, were free to drink on any occasion."

The other glared. "Do you find free to criticize our institutions? Is it not well known that those whom the Supreme has seen fit to place in high position have such heavy burdens upon their shoulders that it is needful for them to seek peace by resort to the holy product of the grape?"

Dean held up a hand, placatingly. "Your Holiness, it is not the desire of myself and my business associates to intrude on the Temple."

"Intrude! My revenues have been cut in half! And what is this new disgusting beverage, ale, so cheap that the most poverty stricken can afford to indulge in it and do so even on feast days, holy days, when wine is traditional?"

Rosetti cleared his throat. "That was the point, Your Holiness. The poor also need their release from their daily pressures. Ale can provide it, at little cost."

"At my expense! That is, of course, at the expense of the Temple."

Dean said, gently, "Your Holiness, it is not our desire to antagonize you." He picked up a quill, dipped it into his ink pot, wrote rapidly on a piece of paper. "Would it help if I made a contribution of... of one million crowns to your, ah, personal account as Presbyter in charge of administering the production and distribution of the, ah, holy product of the vine?"

"One... million... crowns?"

Dean handed him the check.

The Temple father frowned at it. "What is this?"

"A new institution, Your Holiness. If you will present that at any of our recently established banking houses, it will be honored."

Doul scowled at the paper. "I have heard mention of this new institution. And you say this is in value a million crowns?"

"Gold crowns, Your Holiness. A contribution made in recognition of your unfailing labors on behalf of the Temple." Dean found it impossible to keep an edge of sarcasm from his voice.

The other's eyes had narrowed again. He began to say something, but then closed his thin lips to a tight line. He came to his feet. "Very well, my sons." He looked from one of the Earthmen to the other. "Undoubtedly, some meditation on the issues involved is in order."

Dean and Rosetti stood as well. In great ceremony, they saw their visitor to the door.

When they returned to their places, Louis Rosetti was scowling in thought. "You sure that was a good idea, Mike?"

His companion pulled a snowy handkerchief from an inner pocket and wiped his forehead. "I don't know. That molly has had the wine monopoly tied up in his family so long that they think any guzzle is their private preserve."

Rosetti said, "The question is, will he stay bribed?"

"I hope long enough for our new drinks to become so popular he won't be able to blow the whistle on us."

"But suppose he does?"

Dean grinned at him. "A million crowns is a lot of money. That check was made out to Presbyter Doul, personally. When he cashes it, we will have the check. Supposedly, temple monks take the oath of poverty. Our friend Doul is going to look very sick indeed if, on making the charges against us, there are some counter-charges of misappropriating of funds."

Louis Rosetti looked at him doubtfully. "I hope you're not getting too fancy, Mike."

Mike Dean laughed it away.

* * * *

Amschel Mayer was incensed.

"What's got into Buchwald and MacDonald?" he spat.

Jerry Kennedy, attired as was his superior in fur trimmed Genoese robes, signaled one of the servants for a refilling of his glass. Then he shrugged.

"I suppose it's partly our own fault," he said lightly. He sipped the wine the servant had poured from a long-necked dusty bottle and made a mental note to buy up the rest of this vintage for his cellars before young Mannerheim or someone else did.

"Our fault!" Mayer glared. He shook the report he held in his right hand at the other.

The old boy was getting decreasingly tolerant as the years went by, Kennedy decided. He said soothingly, "You sent Peter and Fred over there to speed up local development. Well, that's what they're doing."

"Are you insane?" Mayer squirmed in his chair. "Did you read this radiogram? They've squeezed out all my holdings in rubber, the fastest growing industry on the southern continent. Why, millions are involved. Who do they think they are?"

Kennedy put down his glass and chuckled. "See here, Amschel, we're developing this planet by encouraging free competition. Our contention is that under such socio-economic systems the best men are brought to the lead and benefit all society by the advances they make."

"So! What has this got to do with MacDonald and Buchwald betraying my interests?"

"Don't you see? Using your own theory, you have been set back by someone more efficiently competitive. Fred and Peter saw an opening and, in keeping with your instructions, moved in. It's just coincidence that the rubber they took over was your property rather than some Genoese operator's. If you were open to a loss there, then if they hadn't taken over someone else could have. Possibly Baron Leonar, or even Russ."

"That reminds me," Mayer snapped. "Our Honorable Russ is getting too big for his britches in petroleum. Did you know he's established a laboratory in Amerus? Has a hundred or more chemists working on new products."

Jerry Kennedy finished his wine and motioned to the servant to fill his glass still once again. He said to his older companion, "Fine."

"Fine! What do you mean? Dean is our man in petroleum."

"Look here, if Russ can develop the industry faster than Mike Dean, let him go ahead. That's all to our advantage."

Mayer leaned forward and tapped his assistant emphatically on the knee. "Look here, yourself, Jerome Kennedy. At this stage, we don't want things getting out of our hands. A culture is in the hands of those who control the wealth; the means of production, distribution, communication. Theirs is the real power. I've made a point of spacing our team about the whole planet. Gunther is in mines, Dean heads petroleum among other things, MacDonald shipping, Buchwald steel, Rosetti distilling, Doctor Wieliczka medicine, and so forth. As fast as this planet can assimilate, we push new inventions, new techniques, often whole new sciences, into use. Meanwhile, you and I sit back and dominate it all through the strongest of power mediums, finance."

Jerry Kennedy nodded. "I wouldn't worry about old man Russ taking over Dean's domination of oil, though. Mike's got the support of all the *Pedagogue*'s resources behind him. Besides, we've got to let these Genoese get into the act. The more the economy expands, the more capable men we need. As it is, I think we're already spread a little too thin."

Amschel Mayer had dropped the subject. He was reading the radiogram again and scowling his anger. "This cooks MacDonald and Buchwald. I'll break them."

His assistant took another pull at his drink, and raised his eyebrows. "How do you mean?"

"I'm not going to put up with my subordinates going against my interests."

"In this case, what can you do about it? Business is business."

"You hold quite a bit of their paper, don't you?" The older man's voice held a sly quality.

"You know that. Most of our team's finances funnel through my hands."

"We'll close them out. They've become too concerned with their wealth. They've forgotten why the *Pedagogue* was sent here. I'll break them, Jerry. They'll come crawling. Perhaps I'll send them back to the *Pedagogue*. Make them stay aboard as a permanent crew."

Kennedy shrugged. "Well, Peter MacDonald is going to hate that. He's developed into quite a high playboy—gourmet food, women, one of the most lavish estates on the southern continent."

"Ha!" Mayer snorted. "Let him go back to ship's rations and crews' quarters."

A servant entered the lushly furnished room and announced: "The Honorable Gunther calling on the Honorables Mayer and Kennedy."

"Show him in, of course," Mayer ordered.

Martin Gunther, for once his calm ruffled, hurried into the room. "Rykov," he blurted. "He's disappeared. The barons have probably got him!"

Amschel Mayer shot to his feet. "That's the end," he swore shrilly. "Only in the west have the barons held out. I thought we'd slowly wear them down, take over their powers bit by bit. But this does it. This means we fight!"

He spun to Kennedy. "Jerry, make preparations to take a trip out to the *Pedagogue*. You know the extent of Genoa's industrial progress. Seek out the most advanced weapons this technology could produce."

Kennedy put down his glass, and came to his own feet, shocked by Gunther's words. "But, Amschel, do you think it's wise to start an intercontinental war? Remember, we've been helping to industrialize the west, too. It's almost as advanced as our continent. Their war potential isn't weak."

"Nevertheless," Mayer snapped, "we've got to break the backs of the barons and the Temple monks. Get messages off to Baron Leonar and young Mannerheim, to Russ and Olderman. We'll want them to put pressure on their local politicians. What we need is a continental alliance for this war."

Gunther said, "Should I get in touch with Rosetti and Dean? They're still over there."

Mayer hesitated. "No," he said. "We'll keep Mike and Louis informed but they'd better stay where they are. We'll still want our men in the basic positions of higher power when we've won."

"They might get hurt," Gunther scowled. "The barons might get them too. I'm not so sure about their cover. The Temple's got a lot of strings out. They might know we're all interconnected."

"Nonsense. Mike and Louis can take care of themselves."

Jerry Kennedy was upset. He was not by nature a man of violence. He said, "Are you sure about this war, chief? Isn't a conflict of this size apt to hold up our overall plans?"

"Of course not," Mayer scoffed. "Man makes his greatest progress under pressure. A major war will unite the nations of both the western continent and this one as nothing else could. Both will push their development to the utmost."

He added, thoughtfully, "Which reminds me. It might be a good idea for us to begin accumulating interests in such industries as will be affected by a war economy."

Jerry Kennedy chuckled at him. "Merchant of death."

"What?"

"Nothing," Kennedy said. "Something I read about on an historical tape."

CHAPTER VIII

AT THE DECADE'S END, once again the representatives of the Genoese team were first in the *Pedagogue*'s lounge. Mayer sat at the officers' table, Martin Gunther at his right. Jerry Kennedy leaned against the ship's bar, sipping appreciatively at a highball in a tall glass; the drink was inordinately dark.

They could hear the impact of the spaceboat from Texcoco when it slid into its bed.

"Poor piloting," Gunther mused. "Whoever's doing that flying doesn't get enough practice."

They could hear the ports opening and then the sound of approaching feet. The footsteps had a strangely military ring, for a group of scientists and technicians.

Joe Chessman entered, followed immediately by Barry Watson, Dick Hawkins and Natt Roberts. They were all dressed in heavy uniform, complete with colorful decorations. Behind them were four Texcocans, including Reif and his teenage son, Taller, also in uniform, though the other two Tulans wore civilian dress.

Mayer scowled at them in the way of greeting. "Where's Plekhanov?" he snapped. "The agreement was that the heads of teams meet each decade."

"Leonid Plekhanov is no longer with us," Chessman said sourly. "Under pressure his mind evidently snapped and he made decisions that would have meant the collapse of the expedition. He resisted when we reasoned with him."

The four members of the Genoese team stared without speaking. Jerry Kennedy put down his glass at last. "You mean you had to restrict him? Why didn't you bring him back to the ship?"

Barry Watson said slowly, "He was put under guard. We were in combat. The men who guarded him disappeared in the fray. Leonid evidently died with them. We are lucky any of us survived."

"You should have taken more efficient steps to protect him," Mayer snapped. "I had my differences with Leonid Plekhanov, but, after all, he was second in command of this expedition. I am not at all sure, now that he is gone, who I will appoint to take his place."

Dick Hawkins chuckled softly.

Chessman took a chair at the table. The others assumed standing positions behind him. He said coldly, "I am afraid we'll have to reject your views on the subject. Twenty years ago this expedition split into two groups. My team will accomplish its original mission, its tasks. Your opinions are not needed."

Amschel Mayer glared at the others in hostility but when he spoke again it was on a different subject. He said, "You have certainly come in force this time."

Chessman said flatly, "Save for Mrs. Chessman, that is, Doctor Sanchez, and Steve Cogswell, who have been left behind to hold things together, this is all of us, Mayer."

"All of you? Where are Stevens and MacBride?"

Barry Watson said, "Plekhanov's fault. Lost in the battle that broke the back of the rebels. At least they died in good cause."

Joe Chessman looked at his military chief. "I'll act as team spokesman, Barry."

"Broke the back of the rebels," Jerry Kennedy mused. "That opens all sorts of avenues, doesn't it?"

Chessman growled. "I suppose that in the past twenty years your team had no obstacles. Not a drop of blood shed. Come on, the truth. How many of your team has been lost in this peaceful program of yours?"

Mayer shifted in his chair. "Possibly your point is well taken. Nick Rykov fell into the hands of a group of malcontents, some of the barons and Temple monks who oppose our reforms. Our reports indicate he is dead."

"Only one man lost, eh?"

Mayer stirred uncomfortably then flushed at the other's tone. "Something has happened to Buchwald and MacDonald. They must be insane. They've broken off contact with me, are amassing personal fortunes in the eastern hemisphere."

Hawkins laughed abruptly. "Free competition," he said.

Barry Watson leaned forward and said to Kennedy, rather than to Amschel Mayer. "How is, uh, Doctor Wieliczka? Why didn't she come?"

Kennedy cocked his head questioningly but said, "Too busy. She's got a whole string of medical universities and hospitals under her care. However, she sent you a message."

Watson looked at him. "Well?"

Kennedy said slowly, "She said, give him my love..."

Barry Watson flushed.

"...if he still wants it."

Chessman growled. "Let's halt this bickering and jabber and get to business. First, let me introduce Reif, Texcocan State Army Chief of Staff and his son Taller."

Reif and his son came to a formal salute. The Earthmen from Genoa nodded acknowledgment, uncomfortably.

Chessman said, "And these other Texcocans are Wiss and Foken, both of whom have gone far in the sciences."

The two Tulan scientists shook hands, Earth style, but then stepped to the rear again where they followed the conversation without comment.

Mayer said, "You think it wise to introduce natives to the *Pedagogue*? Last time it was armed guards. This time prominent officials and scientists."

"Of course," Chessman said. "Following this conference I am going to take Foken and Wiss into the library. What are we here for if not to bring these people up to our level as rapidly as possible?"

"Very well," Mayer conceded grudgingly. "And now I have a complaint. When the *Pedagogue* first arrived we had only so many weapons aboard. However, both teams have evidently run into more physical violence than was at first expected. And you have taken more than half of the ship's weapons in the past two decades."

Chessman shrugged it off. "We'll return the greater part to the ship's arsenal. At this stage, we are producing our own."

"I'll bet you are," Jerry Kennedy said. "Look, any of you fellows want a real Earthside whiskey? When we were crewing this expedition, why didn't we bring someone with a knowledge of distilling, brewing and fermenting?"

Mayer snapped at him. "Jerry, you drink too much."

"The hell I do," the other said cheerfully. "Not near enough."

Barry Watson said easily, "A drink wouldn't hurt. Why're we so stiff? This is the first get-together for ten years. Jerry, you're putting on weight."

Kennedy looked down at his rounded stomach. "Don't get enough exercise," he said, then reversed the attack. "You look older, Barry. Are you taking your rejuvenation treatments?"

Barry Watson grimaced. "Sure, but I'm working under pressure. It's been one long campaign."

Kennedy passed around the drinks, thoughtfully refilling his own glass.

Dick Hawkins laughed. "It's been one long campaign, all right. Barry has a house as big as a castle and six or eight—I don't think he knows himself—women in his harem."

Watson flushed, but obviously without displeasure.

Martin Gunther, of the Genoese team, cocked his head. "Harem?"

Joe Chessman said impatiently, "Man adapts to circumstances, Gunther. The wars have lost us a lot of men. Women are consequently in a surplus. If the population curve is to continue upward, it is necessary that a man serve more than one woman. Polygamy is the obvious answer."

Gunther cleared his throat smoothly. "So a man in Barry's position will have as many as eight wives, eh? You must have lost a *good many* men."

Watson grinned modestly. "Everybody doesn't have that many. It's according to your ability to support them, and, also rank has its privileges, as always. Besides, we figure it's a good idea to spread the best seed around. By mixing our blood with the Texcocans we improve the breed."

Behind him, Taller, the Tulan boy, stirred without notice. One of the two scientists looked at his colleague from the side of his eyes, but the faces of both remained expressionless.

Kennedy finished off his highball and began to build another, immediately. He said, "Here we go again. The big potatoes coming to the top."

Watson flushed. "What do you mean by that, Kennedy?"

"Oh, come off it, Barry," Kennedy laughed. "Just because you're in a position to push these people around doesn't make you the prize stud on Texcoco."

Watson elbowed Dick Hawkins to one side in his attempt to get around the table at the other.

Chessman rapped, "Watson! That's enough. Knock it or I'll have you under arrest." The Texcocan team head turned abruptly to Mayer and Kennedy. "Let's stop this nonsense. We've come to compare progress. Let's begin."

The three members of the Genoese team glared back in antagonism, but then Gunther said grudgingly, "He's right. There is no longer amiability between us, so let's forget it. Perhaps when the fifty years are up, things will be different. Now let's merely be businesslike."

"Well," Mayer said, "our report is that progress accelerates. Our industrial potential expands at a rate that surprises even us. In the near future, we'll introduce the internal combustion engine. Our universities still multiply and are turning out technicians, engineers and scientists at an even quicker rate. In several nations, illiteracy is practically unknown and *per capita* production increases almost everywhere." Mayer paused in satisfaction, as though awaiting the others to attempt to top his report.

Joe Chessman said sourly, "Ah, almost everywhere *per capita* production increases. Why *almost?*"

Mayer snapped. "Obviously, in a system of free competition, all cannot progress at once. Some go under."

"Whole nations?"

"Temporarily, whole nations can receive setbacks as a result of defeat in a war, or perhaps due to lack of natural resources. Some nations progress faster than others."

Chessman said in dour satisfaction, "The whole Texcocan State is one great unit. Everywhere the gross product increases. Within the foreseeable future, the standard of living will be excellent."

Jerry Kennedy, an alcoholic lisp in his voice now, said, "You mean you've accomplished the planet-wide government you were telling us about at the last meeting?"

"Well, no. Not as yet." Chessman's sullen voice had an element of chagrin in it. "However, there are no strong elements left that oppose us. We are now pacifying the more remote areas."

"Sounds like a rather bloody program—especially if Barry Watson, here, winds up with eight women," Martin Gunther said.

Watson started to retort to that, but Chessman held up a restraining hand. "The Texcocan State is too strong to be resisted, Gunther. It is mostly a matter of getting around to the more remote peoples. As soon as we bring in a new tribe, we convert it into a commune."

"Commune!" Kennedy blurted.

Joe Chessman raised his thick eyebrows at the other. "The most efficient socio-economic unit at this stage of development. Tribal society is perfectly adapted to fit into such a plan. The principal differences between a tribe and a commune is that under the commune you have the advantage of a State above in a position to give you the benefit of mass industries, schools, medical assistance. In return, of course, for a certain amount of taxes, a military levy and so forth."

Martin Gunther said softly, "I recall reading of the commune system as a student, but I fail to remember the supposed advantages."

Chessman growled. "They're obvious. You have a unit of tens of thousands of persons. Instead of living in individual houses, each with a man working while the woman cooks and takes care of the home and the children, all live in community houses and take their meals in a mess hall. The children are cared for by trained nurses. During the season all able adults go out en masse to work the fields. When the harvest has been taken in, the farmer does not hole up for the winter but is occupied in local industrial projects, or in road or dam building. The commune's labor is never idle."

Kennedy shuddered involuntarily.

Chessman looked at him coldly. "It means quick progress. Meanwhile, we go through each commune and from earliest youth, locate those members who are suited to higher studies. We bring them into state schools where they get as much education as they can assimilate—more than is available in commune schools. These are the Texcocans we are training in the sciences."

"The march to the anthill," Amschel Mayer muttered.

Chessman eyed him scornfully. "You amuse me, old man. You with your talk of building an economy with a system of free competition. Our Texcocans are sacrificing today but their children will live in abundance. Even today, nobody starves, no one goes without shelter or medical care." Chessman twisted his mouth. "We have found that hungry, cold or sick people cannot work efficiently."

He stared challengingly at the Genoese leader. "Can you honestly say the same? That there are no starving people in Genoa? No inadequately housed, no sick without hope of medicine? Do you have economic setbacks in which poorly planned production goes amuck and depressions follow with mass unemployment?"

"Nevertheless," Mayer said, with unwonted calm, "our society is still far ahead of yours. A mere handful of your bureaucratic and military chiefs enjoy the good things of life. There are tens of thousands on Genoa who have them. Free competition has its weaknesses, perhaps, but it provides a greater good for a greater number of persons."

Joe Chessman came to his feet. "We'll see," he said stolidly. "In ten years, Mayer, we'll consider the positions of both our planets once again."

"Ten years it is," Mayer snapped back at him.

Jerry Kennedy saluted with his glass. "Cheers," he said.

* * * *

On the return to Genoa, Amschel Mayer looked his disgust at his right hand man. Kennedy was not piloting the small craft, as usual. Martin Gunther was at the controls.

Mayer said, "Are you sober enough to assimilate something serious?"

Jerry Kennedy shook his head to achieve clarity. "Sure, chief, of course. That Earthside liquor is just a little stronger than what I'm used to these days, I guess. Sneaks up on you."

Mayer grunted contempt but said, "Well then, begin taking the steps necessary for us to place a few men on Texcoco in the way of, ah, intelligence agents."

"You mean some of our team?" Kennedy said, startled.

Gunther looked over from the space launch's controls and raised his eyebrows.

Mayer said impatiently. "No, no of course not. We can't spare them, and, besides, there'd be too big a chance of recognition and exposure. We'll have to use some of our more trusted Genoese. Make the reward enough to attract their services." He looked from one of his lieutenants to the other significantly. "I think you'll agree that it might not be a bad idea to keep our eyes on the developments on Texcoco."

Martin Gunther thought about it. "Well, perhaps, but there's another aspect, Amschel. Thus far, we've kept the secret of the *Pedagogue*'s existence from anybody we come in contact with on Genoa. Not even such close business associates as Mannerheim have been told about the real nature of our mission."

"Ummm, Kennedy said glumly. "And as soon as you start organizing an espionage mission to Texcoco, the fat will be in the fire."

Mayer said, "It will be a top secret. Only a few very trusted, very dependable men will be used. You can ferry them over in this craft. Over there, perhaps, they can make contact with those elements in revolt against Chessman and his team. They can infiltrate one or more of these so-called communes, and keep in touch with whatever real progress Joe and his men are making—if any."

Jerry Kennedy muttered. "One person can keep a secret, sometimes even two can. From then on the likelihood goes down in a geometric progression, and this project will involve dozens before we're through."

Mayer stared at him. "Just who is in command of this expedition, Jerome Kennedy?"

* * * *

On the way back to Texcoco, Barry Watson said to his chief, "What do you think of putting some security men on Genoa, just to keep tabs?"

"Why?"

Watson looked at his fingers, nibbled at a hangnail. "It just seems to me it wouldn't hurt any."

Chessman snorted.

Dick Hawkins said thoughtfully, "I think Barry's right. Mayer and his gang can bear watching. Besides, in another decade or so they'll realize we're going to beat them in this competition. Mayer's ego isn't going to take that. He'd go to just about any extreme to keep from losing face back on Earth."

Natt Roberts said worriedly, "I think they're right, Joe. Certainly it wouldn't hurt to have a few security men over there. My department could train them, then one of us could pilot them over. Spot a few on each of the three continents. Thing to do would be send men with families. Guarantee that there'd not be any defections."

"Well, you never know. There might be opportunities over there."

"I'll make the decisions around here," Chessman growled at them. "Don't forget who Number One is. I'll think about it. It's just possible that you're right, though."

Seated in the stern of the space lighter were the three adult Tulans and Taller, the teenager. Reif let his eyes go from one face to another, but he said nothing.

* * * *

Natalie Wieliczka looked out over the large audience which crowded the auditorium with a certain modest pride. She said, "Very well. That concludes my lecture. Are there any questions?"

One of her listeners came to his feet.

There was a sly element in his voice. "In all your speech today, Honorable Doctor, you have dealt with new methods of controlling the diseases that have ravaged the world for so long, for whatever reason that the Supreme has seen fit in his wisdom. However, never have you mentioned the Temple which has always traditionally been the recourse of the ill. These new methods are other than those utilized by the Temple monks. You say nothing of the holy incantations necessary to supplement medication and other therapy. Is there, then, no place in your teachings for the Supreme?"

There was a snicker that went through the audience which was composed almost exclusively of graduate medical students. Inwardly, Natalie winced at it. The questioner was a plant. That she knew. She was being deliberately provoked.

She tried to brazen it out. She carefully chose her words.

"The Temple deals primarily with your immortal soul, with your relationship with your god, though, of course Temple monks often participate in other matters of interest to the community. Our field, with which we are exclusively concerned, as doctors, is medicine, which deals with the health of the people, on this plane of existence. As doctors, no matter how religious we may be as individuals, we do not deal with the soul or the hereafter."

He was still standing.

He said, "But do you not think it is necessary to have present a Temple monk at any sick bed, in order to invoke the aid of the Supreme?"

Natalie Wieliczka ran the tip of her tongue over her lower lip. "Let us say that it can never do harm to have a representative of the Temple present while a trained doctor of medicine is administering to a patient."

"But is it *necessary?*"

There was a stirring in the audience. A young student called to the questioner: "Sit down, you flat!"

But most of them watched her. Watched her carefully. Waited tensely for her words.

She was at a crossroads and knew it. Now, all bets were down. It had been building for some time and she had long avoided it.

Natalie Wieliczka said very slowly, "No, it is not necessary for a Temple monk to be present." She took a deep breath. "Incantations are not necessary to cure the sick."

"That, Honorable Doctor, is blasphemy!"

She shook her head. The die was cast now. "It is not meant to be."

"Honorable Doctor," the man shouted, "it is well known that you never attend the Temple."

"I am too busy with my work."

"Honorable Doctor, are you afraid to attend the Temple?"

"Certainly not! Are there any other questions?"

A black cloaked figure who had been sitting inconspicuously in the last row of seats, came to his feet. He said, his voice seemingly low, but still it rolled out over the auditorium, "The holy books say that it is impossible for a witch to enter the house of the Supreme without suffering immediate death."

Natalie winced but bit out: "I am not a witch. I am a doctor of medicine. I have never seen a witch." She took a deep breath. "I do not believe that such things as witches exist."

The man in black rumbled. "The holy books also say that the faithful shall not suffer a witch to live."

CHAPTER IX

THOUGH HE WAS NOT aware of the fact, Taller Second was a near duplicate of his grandfather, the Khan of all the People who had first greeted
the Earthmen upon their original arrival in Tula. Taller Second was a
large, very handsome man, born with the air of command, even in his
youth.

Now, in the uniform of a field officer, he strode through the portals of
the hospital, the second largest of the new buildings springing up throughout the city. Even in his own memory, Tula had more than tripled in size.
Its growth had not necessarily coincided with beautification. Primitive
pyramids stood cheek to jowl with rearing distribution centers or office
buildings. Community adobe structures, once inhabited by families be-
longing to the same clans, adjoined modern apartment buildings going up
for the rapidly evolving New Class, the bureaucrats of the State.

Within the building, he looked about. It had been some time since he
had been here. However, he remembered his way.

Though he was the son of Reif and high in the ranks of the Tulans, he
was little known in the hospital and his passage drew small attention. He
strode down one corridor, through a heavy door, down another corridor, to
bring up finally before a guarded portal.

The guard wore a highly decorative tunic and kilts, the design of which
was unfamiliar to Taller, and, somehow, in its finery, repugnant. The other
came to attention, his carbine held athwart his chest.

He snapped briskly. "It is forbidden to enter the private chambers of
the lady of Number One."

Taller looked at the man. He said, finally, "Soldier, do you know who I
am?"

The other looked straight ahead. "Yes, sir."

"Are you sure, soldier?"

"Yes, sir. You are Taller Second, son of the Khan of all the People."

Taller looked at him levelly. "Then, soldier, if I were to ignore you and
pass through this door, what would you do?"

There was a pleading element in the other's expression, even as he
tried to stare straight ahead. The carbine slumped in his hands. He said,
"Sir, it is by command of Number One that I am posted here."

"I didn't ask you that," Taller said.

"No, sir." The other was bewildered.

Taller breathed deeply. He said, "As it is, I am here by invitation, soldier. Go through whatever routine is standard to take me... to take me to the lady of Number One."

In obvious relief, the guard retreated through the door in question, to return almost immediately.

He came to the salute. "Enter the quarters of the lady of Number One, Taller, son of the Khan."

Taller grunted and passed the other.

Inside, he looked about, his eyebrows rising. He had never been here before, although he had heard rumors of the innermost sanctum of Doctor Isobel Sanchez. Being only two generations away from a primitive background, he was poorly prepared to confront the ultra-modern furnishings, art work and atmosphere of Earth.

A serving girl scurried up, her eyes averted, an all but cringing quality in her approach. She was bare-footed, bare above the waist, and her physical qualities were undeniable, indeed; she had obviously been selected for them. She wore nothing save a mini-kilt.

"My lord," she said. "The Doctor awaits you." She began to turn to lead the way.

Taller said, "A moment."

She hesitated and there was a fearful quality.

He looked at her, at her bare bosom, which was superb. The Tulan people were not so far from their primitive past but that they still held to the simple modesty. Taller had never seen a woman's nipples before.

Taller said, "You are of the People?"

"Yes, lord."

"No not call me *lord*. Such is not a term of address to be used to a son of the People. My father is Khan, but the office is elective. Some day I may, in turn, be Khan, but only if the People so decide. We have no lords amongst the People, as you should know."

The girl was apprehensive. Taller was not a man to be stood up to by a wisp of a girl. She said, her eyes down, "But, sir, it is the Doctor's orders that I entitle all her guests lord."

"Why do you go without proper garments?"

The girl was miserable. "It is the orders of the Doctor."

He looked at her for a long moment, grimly. Finally, "Take me to her."

Isobel Sanchez had been reclining on an Etruscan type lounge. Upon his entry, she came to one elbow and shrugged into a jacket which was, however, so diaphanous that it concealed her figure little better than the serving girl's who bowed him in and then quickly bowed herself out.

Taller looked at Isobel Sanchez for a moment, then after the girl. His gray eyes came back to the Earthwoman.

He said, "Why is she so attired?"

Isobel tinkled a laugh. "Because I find it amusing. I call the dress Cretan Revival."

"Cretan?"

"A very old people of First Earth. They developed one of the highest civilizations."

"And became shameless?"

She had come to her feet and now she approached him, amusement in her eyes. "It is an elastic term, Taller. Would you like a drink?" She motioned to a golden ewer. "I have been experimenting. I found in the *Pedagogue*'s archives an account of an old... very old... beverage called absinthe."

Without waiting for his answer, she took up the ewer and poured a greenish liquid from it into two glasses.

He watched her impassively as she went through the ceremony of putting a lump of sugar, on a spoon, above each of the glasses in turn, and then pouring cold water from another jar over the sugar until it dissolved away into the absinthe.

Her figure was rather clearly revealed through the all but transparent clothing she wore. Taller had known this woman all his life, though he had come little in contact with her. So far as he could remember, she had looked like this always. Perhaps she was a shade more lush, an inconsequential, more slack about the mouth, a touch more empty in the eyes— but largely she was the most beautiful woman he could ever remember having seen.

She turned and handed him the glass and stood there, before him, her lips slightly parted.

He drank and didn't like the taste, but said nothing.

Isobel Sanchez looked at him mockingly. "I believe this is your first visit here, Taller."

"Yes. Why did you summon me?"

She sipped at her drink and looked up into his eyes and her own were still mocking. "But you are one of our most important officers."

He frowned at her.

She said slowly, "And I am the planet's leading... doctor. And this is my hospital."

Taller said, "Outside is your hospital, but these are your private quarters. And you are the woman of Number One, Joe Chessman."

She made a pout. "Joe is too busy these days. I seldom see him. When I do, he is always talking about his work. So far as the hospital is concerned, it is no longer necessary for me to do drudgery. My doctors handle that. If something important comes up that they don't understand, they can come to me." She added languidly, "If I have the time. But with you..."

He still frowned.

She put her glass down and looked into his eyes again, and now hers were slumberous. "I think I should give *you* a personal... examination."

His mouth was suddenly dry as she came into his arms.

* * * *

Steve Cogswell sat at a table in a village square. Two Tulan guards bearing rifles flanked him. He alone was seated. Before him stood a long line, patiently, stolidly. Most of the petitioners were men, but not all.

He rubbed a hand around the back of his neck, in thorough weariness, and said, "All right, who's next?"

Before the table and slightly to one side, the apprehensive nonentity who was the village head man read from a paper. The next in line stepped forward.

"All right," Cogswell sighed. "What's your crab?"

The newcomer was in his middle years. There was a stupid, dull quality in his face. His body was obviously strong, but bent with the years.

He rumbled. "You have taken my land."

Cogswell shook his head. "You don't understand. I have taken nothing from you. I merely represent the State. The State, itself, has actually taken nothing from you, in reality. The land still belongs to you, to you and all the others who work it."

"I had ten hectares. It was my father's before me, and his father's. My sons and I worked it." He held out grimy hands, worn with toil, the nails broken. "We worked it with our hands and earned our living. Now you have taken it."

Steve Cogswell took a deep breath.

"Look, man. Your land and all the other land in this vicinity has been amalgamated, joined together. You'll work it in common. It will be easier. You won't have to work from morning till night. You'll put in six or eight hours a day, no more. We're bringing in fertilizer; soon there will be tractors, other machinery. Using a third the amount of labor, you'll be producing more agricultural products. We're not taking anything from you, we're giving you something."

"They tell me that my house is to be destroyed. That it is to be cleared away, so that this new machinery can have room. It is my house, where I was born, where my sons were born."

"I know. I know," Cogswell growled. "And your father, and his father before him. I've heard the story a thousand and one times. How many

85

rooms were there in this house?"

The petitioner looked at him blankly. "One room above for we of the family, one room below for the animals. As all houses in this region."

Cogswell looked at the village headman. "Hasn't it been explained to everyone that they will be moved into the village? That new apartments with several rooms apiece, and bathrooms and kitchens, will be provided?"

The headman said, "All have been told this, but thus far few of these apartments have been built. Even those who have been provided with such apartments, do not like them, Man from First Earth. They like their old homes, the houses such as their ancestors have always lived in."

Steve Cogswell closed his eyes in pain. "What's wrong with the new apartments? They're sanitary. They're comparatively spacious. We're introducing gas stoves. What in the name of Holy Jumping Zen do these cloddies want?"

The headman said unctuously, "Man from First Earth, they want what they are used to. When a family moves into one of the new apartments, they pull down the interior walls so that the whole house can be one room. They are not used to the home being many rooms, it prevents the family from being one. This new soap that comes from the new industrial centers, the growing cities. We are not used to this soap. It is not well that the People wash themselves all the time, such as you suggest. Only on feast days, on holy days did we bathe in the past."

"Yes," Cogswell muttered bitterly. "I remember the smell."

He looked back at the farmer. "Listen," he said, "the world changes. It changes for the better."

"I do not want these changes. Already one of my sons has left the village and gone to Tula to work in the new projects. He should be here with the rest of us, working the fields, tending the animals. It is not..."

Cogswell held up a hand. "Look. That's the point. The changes we are making will make it possible to release workers from the fields so that they can get positions in the new industries. Everybody will profit by these new industries. You'll have more and better food; there'll never be famines again. You'll have better clothes, better transportation, better medicine."

"We do not want these things," the other said stubbornly. "We want to continue in the old way. We want our land. It is our land. It is not yours to take."

"*I'm* not taking it," Cogswell snapped impatiently. "Zen! Can't you understand? The *State* is taking it."

"I do not understand about this State of which you talk. I am a simple man. I do not want you to take my land. Where will my sons bring their wives when they are of age to wed?"

"The State is everybody," Cogswell told him. "When your sons marry, they'll be given apartments here in town. Each day they will be driven out to the farmland to work. They'll live in luxury, compared to the way you always have. Holy Zen, man! Can't you see this is for your own good?"

Without waiting for an answer, Cogswell looked at the headman. "Who's next? I'm getting tired of these cloddies! Over and over again, the same confounded drivel!"

The peasant hadn't stirred. He was breathing deeply now. He pressed closer to the table behind which the Earthman sat.

"The land is ours!"

Cogswell leaned forward too, his face red with anger. "The land is now the State's, whether you like it or not!"

The two guards, bored with the monotony, moved too slowly. They hadn't expected action.

The knife came from nowhere, concealed perhaps in sleeve or jerkin folds.

The guards clubbed their rifles, struck again and again. Beat the man to the ground and senseless. Beat him long after consciousness was gone.

Not that this made any difference to Steven Cogswell, once of New Chicago in a land far, far from Texcoco. Already, his body was growing cold.

A deep sigh went through the long line of farmer petitioners. The headman, his eyes popping horror, was terrified. Word of the brutality of the new police was spreading throughout the countryside.

* * * *

Down the long palace corridor strode Barry Watson, Dick Hawkins, Natt Roberts, the aging Reif and his son Taller, now in the prime of manhood. Their faces were equally lined from long hours without sleep. Half a dozen armed Tulan infantrymen brought up their rear.

As they passed Security Police guards, to left and right, eyes took in their weapons, openly carried. But such eyes shifted and the guards remained at their posts. Only one sergeant opened his mouth in protest. "Sir," he said to Watson, hesitantly, "you are entering Number One's presence armed."

"Shut up," Natt Roberts rapped at him.

Reif said, "That will be all, sergeant."

The Security Police sergeant looked emptily after them as they progressed down the corridor.

Together, Watson and Reif motioned aside the two Tulan soldiers who stood before the door of their destination, and pushed inward without knocking.

Joe Chessman looked up wearily from his map and dispatch-laden desk. For a moment his hand went to the heavy military revolver at his right but when he realized the identity of his callers, it fell away. Isobel Sanchez, as always, lush, sat in an easy chair on the far side of the room, her face petulant, a drink in her hand.

She grunted contemptuously. "Another big crisis, without doubt. I tell you, I'm getting tired of being cooped up in this place."

"What's up now?" Joe Chessman said, his voice on the verge of cracking.

The men hadn't even bothered to look at the woman. Their eyes were on Chessman. Barry Watson acted as spokesman.

"It's everywhere the same. The communes are on the fine edge of revolt. They've been pushed too far. They've got to the point where they just don't give a damn. A spark and all Texcoco goes up in flames."

Reif said coldly, "We need immediate reforms. They've got to be pacified. An immediate announcement of more consumer goods, fewer State taxes, above all a relaxation of Security Police pressures. Given immediate promise of these, we might maintain ourselves."

Joe Chessman's sullen face was twitching at the right corner of his mouth. Taller Second made no attempt to disguise his contempt at the other's weakness in time of stress.

Chessman's eyes went around the half circle of them. "This is the only alternative? It'll slow up our heavy industry-planned program. I wanted to concentrate everything on steel. Otherwise, we might not catch up with Genoa as quickly as we figured."

Barry Watson gestured with a hand in quick irritation. "Look here, Chessman, don't we get through to you? Whether or not we build up a steel capacity as large as Amschel Mayer's isn't important now. Simple survival is. Everything's at stake."

"Don't talk to me that way, Barry," Chessman growled truculently. "I'll make the decisions. I'll do the thinking around here." He looked at Reif in speculation. "How much of the Tulan army is loyal—to me?"

The aging Tulan looked at Watson before turning back to Joe Chessman. "All of the Tulan army is loyal—to me."

Evidently, Joe Chessman hadn't picked up the final two words, or, if so, he ignored them. "Good!" he said. He pushed some of the dispatches on his desk aside, letting them flutter to the floor. He bared a field map. "If we crush half a dozen of the local communes... crush them hard! Then the others..."

Watson said very slowly and so low as hardly to be heard, "You didn't bother to listen, Chessman. We told you, all that's needed is a spark."

Isobel said, "Joe, honey, you don't have to take that tone of voice from Barry." She sloshed some more fluid into her glass from a decanter on the small table next to her.

They all ignored her.

Joe Chessman sat back in his chair, looked at them all again, one by one. Re-evaluating. For a moment, the facial tic stopped and his eyes held the old alertness.

"I see," he said. "And you all recommend capitulation to the demands of these potential rebels?"

"It's our only chance," Hawkins said. "We don't even know it'll work. There's always the chance if we throw them a few crumbs they'll want the whole loaf. You've got to remember that some of them have been living for twenty-five years or more under this pressure. The valve is about to blow."

"I see," Chessman grunted. "And what else? I can see in your faces there's something else."

The three Earthmen didn't answer. Their eyes shifted.

Joe Chessman looked to young Taller and then to Reif. "What else?" he demanded.

"We need a scapegoat," Reif said without expression.

Joe Chessman thought about that. He looked at Barry Watson again.

Isobel said petulantly, "What'ya mean, a scapegoat?"

"Shut up," Chessman growled.

Watson said, "The whole Texcocan State is about to topple. Not only do we have to give them immediate reform, but we're going to have to blame the past hardships and mistakes on somebody. Somebody has to take the rap, be thrown to the wolves. If not, maybe we'll all wind up taking the blame."

"Ah," Chessman said. His red-rimmed eyes went around them again, thoughtfully. "We should be able to dig up a few local chieftains and some of the Security Police heads. Or, would it be better to drag some of the old rebels out of the concentration camps and give them a big public trial? Accuse them of sabotaging the State's plans."

They shook their heads.

"What's all this about?" Isobel said petulantly. "What're you all talking about so grimly. Let's all have a nice big drink. It's too glum around this damn palace."

"It has to be somebody big," Natt Roberts said thickly. "A few of my Security Police won't do it."

Joe Chessman's eyes went to Reif. "The Khan is the highest ranking Texcocan of all," he said, finally. "The Khan and some Security Police heads would satisfy them."

Reif's face was as frigid as the Earthman's. He said, "I am afraid not, Joseph Chessman. You are Number One. It is your statue that is in every commune square. It is your portrait that hangs in every distribution center, every mess hall, every schoolroom. You are the Number One—as you have so often pointed out to us. My title, Khan of all the People, has become meaningless."

Isobel shrilled. "Joel Call your guards!"

Joe Chessman spat out a curse, fumbled the gun into his hand and fired before the Tulan soldiers could get to him. In a moment they had wrested the weapon from his hand and had his arms bound. It was too late.

Reif had been thrown backward two paces by the blast of the heavy calibered gun. Now he held a palm over his belly and staggered to a chair. He collapsed into it, looked at his son, let a wash of amusement pass over his face, said, "Khan," meaninglessly, and died.

Isobel, squealing dismay, scurried from her chair and to his side. She knelt, her hands went out, suddenly professional.

She looked up, a strangeness in her eyes. "He's dead," she said.

Natt Roberts shrilled at Chessman: "You fool! We were going to give you a big, theatrical trial. Sentence you to prison, and then, later, claim you'd died in your cell and smuggle you out to the *Pedagogue*."

Watson snapped to the guards. "Take him outside and shoot him!"

Isobel, her eyes wide, put the back of her hand to her mouth. "Barry!" she squealed.

The Tulans began dragging the snarling, cursing Chessman to the door.

Taller said, "A moment, please."

Watson, Roberts, Hawkins and Isobel Sanchez looked at him.

Taller said, "This, perhaps, can be done more effectively."

His voice was completely emotionless. "This man has killed both my father and grandfather, both of them Khans of Tula, elected heads of the most powerful city on all Texcoco, before the coming of you from First Earth."

The guards hesitated. Barry Watson detained them with a motion of his hand.

Taller said, "I suggest you turn him over to me, to be dealt with in the traditional way of the People."

"No," Chessman said hoarsely. "Barry, Dick, Natt. Send me back to the *Pedagogue*. I'll be out of things there. Or maybe Mayer can use me on Genoa."

They didn't bother to look in his direction. Roberts muttered savagely, "We told you, all that was needed was a spark. Now you've killed the Khan, the most popular man on Texcoco. There's no way of saving you."

Isobel's eyes were darting. They were narrowed and speculative.

Taller said, "None of you have studied our traditions, our customs. But now, perhaps, you will understand the added effect of my taking charge. It will be more... profitable. This manner of using the downfall of this... this powermad murderer."

Chessman said desperately, "Look, Barry, Natt. If you have to, shoot me. At least give me a man's death. Remember those human sacrifices the Tulans had when we first arrived? Can you imagine what went on in those temples? Barry, Dick—for old time's sake, boys!"

Barry Watson said to Taller, "He's yours. If this doesn't take the pressure off us, nothing will."

CHAPTER X

MIKE DEAN was on the run.

Swearing, he flung open the door of his office and barged through. He came to an abrupt halt. His secretary, Lange, was bent over the heavy ornate iron safe that sat in one corner. The other heard him, swung around quickly, a hand streaking for a pocket.

Dean's gun was out first, but he didn't fire.

He said breathlessly, "The rats are deserting, eh? Don't bring that shooter out, Lange."

The secretary stood erect. "What do you want?"

Mike Dean grunted cynical amusement. "Evidently the same thing you do. Get over against that wall."

The Earthman came up behind the other and nudged him with the short-barreled gun. "Lean up against the wall with both hands, your legs spread, you funker."

The secretary snarled. "You can't do this!"

Dean snorted wry amusement again. "Famous last words," he muttered. He quickly frisked the other, relieving the man of his weapon. Dean slipped it into one of his own pockets.

He went over to the safe and brought forth several heavy leather purses. "For emergencies only," he said to nobody in particular. He put three of them into his clothing, scowled down at two more. He shook his head. "They'd just weigh me down," he muttered. "And I'd probably not have any use for it anyway."

He went over to the window and stared down into the streets, his lips thinning back over his teeth. "Zen!" he growled. "Here come the boys."

He turned back to Lange and looked at him thoughtfully. "You knew this was going to happen, didn't you? Why ask, you funker? You must have been the one that turned my papers over to the barons and the Temple. Get out of those clothes."

The other was startled. "Why?"

"I said get out of those clothes. You're the most inconspicuously dressed cloddy in town. Get out of those clothes, before I use this shooter on you."

Mike Dean withdrew to the far end of the office and began rapidly to strip his own body of its rich attire. Lange, slowly, reluctantly, began to do the same.

Dean snarled: "Hurry it up or I'll strip them off your dead body."

Lange sped up the operation.

"All right, now get up against the wall over here. Same position as before. And don't get any silly ideas. I can get this shooter into operation quicker than you have any idea."

Mike Dean hurriedly dressed himself in the secretary's conservative garb, remembering at the last moment to transfer his emergency purses to the new pockets. Already, in the outer offices he could hear sounds. He had a few moments. There were several locked doors, heavy, massive doors, between himself and the newcomers. He darted his eyes around the room. At the safe, at his desk. But he shook his head, so that his jowls trembled. He had insufficient time.

He looked at Lange, thoughtfully and brought up his gun.

"No. No, don't do it," the other shrilled in terror. "I won't betray you. I won't talk."

Mike Dean snarled at him. The noises from without the heavy office door were growing in magnitude. "I haven't got the heart," he growled in self disgust.

Mike Dean hurried over to the back entrance, held his gun at the ready and flung the door open. There was nobody beyond. He hurried through into the corridor.

Behind him, Lange scurried to the opposite door, twisted the key. He opened the portal wide.

"He's in here! He was just in here!" he screamed.

Two men at arms hurried in, guns in hand. They stared at the almost nude secretary.

Lange said shrilly, "He went that way." He pointed excitedly. "He stole all my clothes. He went through there."

More men crowded into the room. Several followed the pointing Lange's directions, hurrying after the escaping tycoon.

Presbyter Doul came in, his eyes sweeping the office. They lit on the open safe. They came back to the secretary.

"It would seem that the vultures already gather," the monk murmured.

"No," Lange protested. "It wasn't me. It was him. But he took only some gold crowns. Several purses of them. Everything else is still there."

"It had better be," Doul muttered, heading for the safe.

* * * *

Mike Dean darted down a narrow alleyway, cobblestones under his feet. This town resembled nothing so much as a scene of a medieval city, in the historical Tri-Di cinema back on Earth. He had the feeling of being an actor in a third rate production.

He could hear a scrambling of feet behind him, and turned and winged three shots back. The scrambling stopped. Undoubtedly, the other had slipped into the shelter of a doorway.

Dean hurried on.

He was weighing chances in the back of his mind even as he devoted most of his thoughts to the immediate problem of staying alive. His chances didn't weigh up to much. He had been a fool. He and Louis Rosetti both. They should have allowed for this contingency. Should have figured out some sort of foolproof getaway and hideaway for just such an emergency. They should have realized that you could push opponents just so far, no further.

He rounded a corner. And heard feet behind him again.

Zen! If he had just had another twenty-four hours or so for preparation. He could have gotten to his yacht. It was as fast as anything in any navy on Genoa. He could have gotten to the Eastern continent and to the protection of Amschel Mayer and Jerry Kennedy. They had their continent sewed up to an extent far and beyond what Dean and Rosetti had been able to establish here.

For the nonce he seemed to have shaken his pursuers. They weren't as many as all that, probably. The others were out to get him, true enough, but even more important, they were out to take his properties and undoubtedly were more concerned for them than for his hide.

He didn't dare attempt to secure transportation. Not even a horse. He hurried into another alley, hoping that his sense of direction wasn't playing him false.

Finally, he emerged from a narrow street to confront the large building which was his immediate goal. His eyes darted up and down. The square before him was largely empty. He pushed the gun into his belt, beneath the jerkin he had appropriated from Lange and strolled across, taking on as careless an attitude as he could muster, and trying to keep from breathing in his physical exhaustion in such wise as to draw attention.

He entered the front portals of the building, walked past the receptionist nurse, who gave him no more than a glance, when he projected the air of someone who knew where he was going.

Mike Dean had been here before. He proceeded down the hospital corridor as fast as he could without drawing undue attention.

He didn't bother to knock at her door. He pushed his way through. The nurse at the desk there recognized him and made a standard greeting, but he muttered at her and opened the door to the inner sanctum.

Natalie Wieliczka looked up, surprised at the unheralded intrusion. For a moment she stared. "Mike," she said. "What are you doing in those clothes? I'm used to you as quite the dandy."

Mike Dean went to the window and stared out at the street. He snapped: "Louis is dead."

"What!"

He looked bake at her. "Everything has gone to pot, Natalie. The barons and the Temple have united. They're out to get us all. I think I was able to send a message through to Buchwald and MacDonald. We've got to get out of here, soonest. Have you got a shooter?"

"Me? A gun?" She was still staring, unbelieving.

"Here." He brought the small weapon he had taken from Lange from his pocket and tossed it to her. She grabbed, fumbled, stared down at it.

"Why, why..."

"Come on," he said urgently. "Let's get going."

"But, but Mike. What's the charge against us?" She was aghast.

He looked at her. "Witchcraft."

She closed her eyes and shuddered. "I thought we had wiped that accusation out."

"Well, the Temple's revived it, evidently. They got Louis Rosetti, and they're after me. Obviously, you'd be next. Those Temple monks aren't flats, they've put two and two together and figured out what's happened to a lot of the power they used to have. Come on, Natalie, we've got to try and get out of this city, and some way to get to a ship."

She dithered. "But, my papers. My records."

"Look, don't be a yoke. We have no time, no time for anything." He pointed out the window at a fast running contingent of men, headed by a black-robed Temple monk. "Here they come."

At last she hustled to her feet. She stared out the window. "But I'm a doctor. I haven't broken any laws."

He looked at her glumly. "My dear, a doctor tied to a stake burns just as merrily as does any witch. Is there a back exit out of here?"

She led the way, the small gun clutched, forgotten, in her left hand. She took him out a rear entrance, into the whiteness of a hospital corridor which stretched the full length of the building.

They hurried down it, ignoring the stares of hospital personnel and patients.

Suddenly, the far end of the corridor filled with uniformed men.

"Quick," Dean snapped. "This way!" He branched off into a side hall, she immediately after him. He was puffing. The weight he had taken on over these years as a prosperous tycoon was taking its toll.

They burst through a door and he collided with a burly sergeant of foot, half a dozen of his men bringing up the rear.

Mike Dean was no coward. His gun came up and his face twisted into a snarl.

Natalie Wieliczka grabbed his arm, dragging the gun down. She had dropped her own weapon.

"Let me go!" he snarled, trying to shake her off. The sergeant evidently had no idea his quarry was so near. He stared, for the moment, motionless.

Natalie said, "No. No, Mike. No killing. We're caught. We can't get away."

More men at arms crowded into the area before them. Behind, they could hear still more coming up.

Mike Dean shrugged. The game was obviously up. Suddenly, he felt very tired. Not just physically so. He wished that he could have somehow got Natalie away, but evidently not even that was in the cards.

The sergeant gathered himself. "You are both under arrest."

Behind him a Temple monk hurried up, his face in great excitement. "In the name of the Supreme..." he began.

"And all that jetsam," Mike Dean muttered.

* * * *

At the end of the third decade, the Texcocan delegation was already seated in the *Pedagogue*'s lounge when Jerome Kennedy, Martin Gunther, Peter MacDonald, Fredric Buchwald and three Genoese, Baron Leonar and the Honorables Russ and Modrin appeared.

The Texcocan group consisted of Barry Watson, Dick Hawkins, and Natt Roberts to one side of him, Taller and six Texcocans on the other.

All came to their feet when the Genoese delegation appeared. Barry Watson was frowning unhappily. He said to Kennedy, "Didn't Doctor Wieliczka come?"

It was MacDonald who answered. He said softly, "Natalie Wieliczka, along with Mike Dean and Louis Rosetti were captured. From what we understand..."

"Captured!" Watson barked. "What happened? What steps have you taken to rescue..."

MacDonald held up a chubby hand. "Evidently, they were burned as witches."

Barry Watson sank into a chair, staring. "Oh, no," he whispered.

Fredric Buchwald's eyes had been going over the Texcocan delegation. "And Doctor Sanchez?"

Dick Hawkins growled. "That bitch is under confinement, House arrest, I suppose you'd call it."

Barry Watson got control of himself. He looked up, his face hard now. "Where's Amschel Mayer? I've got some important points to cover with him."

All began to find seating for themselves, Kennedy saying Barry Watson in a slur, "Take it easy fella. For that matter where's Joe Chessman?"

Watson glared at the other. "You know where he is."

"That I do, that I do," Kennedy chuckled. "He's purged, use a term of yesteryear. At the rate you laddy-bucks are going, there won't be anything left of you by the time our half century is up." He snapped his fingers and a Genoese servant who'd been inconspicuously in the background, hurried to his side. "Let's have some refreshments here. What'll very body have?"

"You act as though you've had enough already," Watson bit out. He was a far cry from the youthful seeming, lanky and easy going man who had landed on Texcoco thirty years before.

Jerry Kennedy ignored him, insisted on everyone being served before he allowed the conversation to turn serious. Both the native Texcocans and those of Genoa eyed each other curiously; both held their peace. Their difference in costume, one group military, the other obviously businessmen, was striking.

Kennedy said slyly, "I see we've been successful in apprehending all of your agents, or you'd know more of our affairs."

"Not all our agents," Watson barked. "Only those on your southern continent. What happened to Amschel Mayer?"

Peter MacDonald, who, with Buchwald, was for the first time attending one of the decade-end conferences, had been hardly recognized in his new girth by the Texcocan team. But his added weight had evidently done nothing to his keenness of mind, although he was evidently somewhat taken back by the degree of animosity in the relationship between the two teams. He said now, smoothly, "Our good Amschel is under arrest. Imprisoned, in fact." He shook his head, his double chins wobbling. "A tragedy."

"Imprisoned!" Taller scowled. "By whom? I don't like this. After all, he was your expedition's headman."

Barry Watson shot the military man an irritated glance but then rapped at MacDonald: "Yes. Don't leave us there. What happened to him?"

MacDonald explained, even as Kennedy, who had already finished his long drink, signaled the servant for another round.

"The financial and industrial empire he had built was overextended. A small crisis and it collapsed. Thousands of investors suffered." The fat man cleared his throat. "Those who were so unfortunate as not to be able to get out from under in time. However, in brief, he was arrested and found guilty."

Barry Watson was unbelieving. "There is nothing you can do? The whole team? Obviously, you're among those who were able to get out from under. Couldn't you bribe him out? Rescue him by force and get him back here to the ship? With all the wealth you characters control..."

Jerry Kennedy laughed shortly. "We were busy bailing ourselves out of our own situations, Watson. You don't know what international finances can be. Besides he dug his own grave... uh, that is, he made his own bed."

Natt Roberts had been watching the Genoese contingent thoughtfully. He said, "It occurs to me that you're the very ones that pulled the rug from under Amschel. You sold him out and took over his position."

"Now, that's an original thought," Fredric Buchwald muttered. "But who would have ever thought of it before Natt? You always were quick with a new idea, Natt."

The two teams were glaring at each other. That is, the Earthmen were. The Genoese and Texcocan native delegates were bright of eye, but otherwise expressionless.

Kennedy took his fresh drink from the waiter. He said, "Let's cut out this dismal talk. How about our progress reports?"

"Progress reports," Barry Watson growled. "That's a laugh. You have your agents on Texcoco, we have our agents on Genoa. What's the use of having these conferences at all?"

For the first time, one of the Genoese put in a word. Baron Leonar, son of the original Baron who had met with Amschel Mayer thirty years before, was a man in his mid-forties. He said quietly, "It seems to me that the time has arrived when the two planets might profit by open intercourse. Surely in this time one has progressed beyond the other in one or more fields, but lagged in others. If I understand it all correctly, the mission of the *Pedagogue* is to bring us to as high a technological level as possible in half a century. Already three decades have passed. Cooperation is now in order."

The Texcocans studied him thoughtfully, but Jerry Kennedy waved in negation with the Land that held his glass. "You don't get it, Baron. You see, the thing is we wanta find out what system is going to do the most the quickest. If we cooperate with Barry's gang, everything'll get all mixed up."

The Honorable Russ, now a wizened man of at least seventy, but still sharply alert, said, "However, Texcoco and Genoa might both profit."

Kennedy grinned at him and said happily, "What do we care? You gotta take the long view. What we're working out here is gonna be used on half a million planets eventually." He tried to snap his fingers. "These two lousy planets don't count that much." He succeeded in snapping them on the second try. "Not that much."

Barry Watson said in disgust, "You're stoned, Jerry."

"Why not?" Kennedy grinned. "Finally perfected a decent brandy. It was like pulling teeth. Lot'sa problems. Like casks to char to age the stuff. No oak on this curd of a world of ours. Had'ta improvise. Great stuff now. Something like Earthside Metaxa. I'll have to send you a few cases, Barry."

"And how would you go about that, Jerry?" Watson said softly.

Kennedy chortled. "Don't be a yoke, Barry. Our space lighter makes a trip to Texcoco every month or so. Must keep up with you boys and what you're doing. Maybe throw a wrench in the works once inna while."

Peter MacDonald said, "Shut up, Jerry. You talk too much."

"Don't talk to me that way," Kennedy sneered. "You'll find yourself having one helluva time floating that loan you need next month. How about another drink everybody? This party's dead."

Watson said, "How about the progress reports? Briefly, we've all but completed our unifying of Texcoco. Minor setbacks have sometimes deterred us, but the march of progress goes on. We..."

"Minor setbacks," Kennedy chortled. "Must have had to bump off five million of the poor slobs before that peasant revolt on the communes was finished with."

Watson said coldly, "We always have a few reactionaries, religious fanatics, misfits, crackpots and malcontents to deal with. However, these are not important. Our industrial potential has finally begun to roll. We doubled steel production this year and will do the same next year. Our hydroelectric installations tripled in the past two years. Coal production is four times higher, lumber production six times. We expect to increase the grain harvest forty percent next season. And..."

The Honorable Russ put in gently, "Please, Honorable Watson, your percentage figures are impressive only if we know from what basis you start. If you produced but five million tons of steel last year, then your growth to ten million is very good but it is still not a considerable amount for an entire planet."

Buchwald said dryly, "If our agents are correct, Texcoco steel production is something like a quarter of our own. I assume that your other basic products are at about the same stage of development."

Watson flushed. "The thing to remember is that our economy continues to grow each year. Yours spurts and stops, jerks ahead a few steps, then grinds to a halt or even retreats. Everything comes to a pause if you few on the top stop making a profit; all that counts in your economy is making money for you stutes in the saddle. Which reminds me. How in the world did you ever get out of that planet-wide depression you were in three years ago?"

Peter MacDonald grunted his disgust. "Planet-wide depression, indeed. A small recession. A temporary readjustment due to over-extension in certain economic and financial fields. It was more a matter of the economy moving sideways for a time. We have built-in guards against any such thing as a depression in the old sense."

From the other side of the table, Dick Hawkins laughed at him. "Where'd you pick up that line of gobbledegook, Peter? You sound as though you've been prowling the *Pedagogue*'s library, looking up the old apologists."

Peter MacDonald came to his feet in indignation. "I don't have to put up with this sort of impudence," he snapped. "What do you know about economics? That ridiculous collectivized society you've jerrybuilt over on Texcoco is proof enough that you're incompetent to have intelligent opinions."

Watson lurched to his own feet. "Nor do we have to listen to your snide cracks about the real progress Texcoco is making, MacDonald. We know what's being accomplished there and we're the ones doing it."

He glared around at his associates. "We don't seem to be making any progress around here," he snapped. "Hawkins, Taller, Roberts! Let's go. Ten years from now, we'll be back and there'll be another story to tell. Even a blind man will be able to see the difference by then."

They marched down the *Pedagogue*'s corridor toward their space lighter, their military boots clanging loud on the bare metal of the floors.

Kennedy called after them: "Ten years from now every family on Genoa'll have a car. Wait'll you see. Television, too. We're introducing TV next year. An' civil aviation. Be all over the place in two, three years...."

The Texcocans slammed the spaceport after them.

Kennedy sloshed some more drink into his glass. "Slobs can't stand the truth," he explained to the others. "Bunch of cloddies."

CHAPTER XI

WITH THE EXCEPTION of a few additional delegates of high ranking Texcocan and Genoese political and scientific heads, the line-up at the end of forty years was the same as ten years earlier—except for the absence of Jerry Kennedy.

Extra tables had been set up and chairs to accommodate the added numbers. To one side were the Genoese: Martin Gunther, Fredric Buchwald, Peter MacDonald with such repeat delegates as Baron Leonar and the Honorables Modrin and Russ and half a dozen newcomers. On the other were Barry Watson, Dick Hawkins and Natt Roberts, Taller and such Texcocans as the scientists Wiss and Foken, army heads, Security Police officials and other notables. All of the Texcocan delegation were in uniform, even the scientists.

Notepads had been placed before each of them and both Barry Watson and Martin Gunther were equipped with gavels.

While chairs were still being shuffled, Barry Watson said over the table to Gunther, "Jerry?"

Martin Gunther shrugged. "Jerry Kennedy is, ah, indisposed." He hesitated, then added, "As a matter of fact, he's at one of the mountain sanitariums, taking a cure. He'll be all right."

Dick Hawkins said grudgingly, "Good. We've lost too many."

Watson pounded with his gavel. "Let's come to order. Gunther, do you have anything to say in the way of preliminaries?"

The other shook his head. "Not especially. I believe we all know where we stand, including the newcomers from Genoa and Texcoco. In brief, this is the fourth meeting of the Earth teams that were sent to these two planets to bring backward colonists to an industrialized culture. It would seem that we are both succeeding—possibly at different rates. Forty years have passed. Ten remain to us."

For a moment there was silence as those present thought back over the years.

Finally, Natt Roberts said, "Possibly you have already discovered this, through your agents, but we have released the information on prolonging of life."

Peter MacDonald, heavier than ever, wheezed, "We too were pressured into such a step."

Baron Leonar said, "And why not?"

Taller, across the table from the Genoa merchant, nodded his stern face in agreement.

Martin Gunther tapped twice on the table with his gavel. "The basic reason for our meeting is to report progress and to reconsider the possibilities of new elements having entered into the situation which might cause us to re-examine our policies. I think we already have a fairly good idea of each other's development." His voice went wry. "At least our agents do a fairly good job of reporting yours."

"And ours, yours," Barry Watson rapped.

"However," MacDonald said, "now that we are drawing near the end of our half century, I think it becomes obvious that Amschel Mayer's original contention—that a freely competitive economy grows faster than one restricted by totalitarian bounds—has been proven."

Barry Watson snorted amusement. "Do you?" he said. "To the contrary, MacDonald. The proof is otherwise. On Genoa you still have comparative confusion. True enough, several of your nations, particularly those on your eastern continent, are greatly advanced and with a high living and cultural standard—when times are good. But at the same time you have other whole peoples who are little, if any, better off than when you arrived. On the southern continent, you even have a few feudalistic regimes that are probably worse off, largely as a result of the wars you've crippled them with."

Natt Roberts took it up, his voice musing. "But even that isn't the important thing. The Co-ordinator sent us here to find a *method* of bringing backward cultures to industrialization. Have you got a blueprint to show him when you return? Can you trace out the history of Genoa for this past half century and say, this war was necessary for progress—but that war should have been avoided? Or is this whole free competition program of yours actually nothing but chaos which *sometimes* works out wonderfully well for *some* nations but actually destroys others? You have scorned our methods, our collectivized society—but when we return, we'll have a blueprint of how we arrived where we are."

Gunther banged the table with his gavel. "Just a moment. Is there any particular reason why we have to listen to these accusations when..."

Watson held up a hand curtly. "Let us finish. If you have something to say, we'll gladly listen when we're through."

Gunther was flushed but he snapped, "Go ahead then, but don't think any of us Genoese are being taken in."

Barry Watson said, "True enough, it took us a time to unite our people..."

"Time and blood," Peter MacDonald muttered under his breath.

"...but once under way, the Texcocan State has moved on in a progression unknown in any of the Genoese nations. To industrialize a society you must reach a certain taking off point, a point where you have sufficient industry, particularly steel, sufficient power, sufficient scientists, technicians and skilled workers. Once that point has been reached you can move ahead in almost a geometric progression. You build a steel mill and with the steel produced you build two more mills the following year, which in turn gives you the material for four the next year."

Fredric Buchwald grunted his disbelief.

Watson looked up and down the line of Genoese, the Earthmen as well as the natives. "On Texcoco we have now reached that point. We have a trained, eager population of over one billion persons. Our universities are turning out highly trained effectives at the rate of more than twenty millions a year. We have located all the raw materials we will need. We are now under way." He looked at them in scornful amusement. "By the end of the next decade, we will bury you."

Martin Gunther said calmly, "Are you through?"

"Yes. For the time," Watson nodded.

"Very well. Then this is *our* progress report. In the past forty years, we have eliminated feudalism in all the more advanced countries. Even in the remote areas the pressures of our changing world are bringing them around. The populous of these countries will no longer stand to one side while the standard of living on the rest of Genoa grows so rapidly. On most of our planet, already the average family not only enjoys freedom, but a way of life far in advance of that of Texcoco. Already modern housing and household appliances are everywhere. Already both land cars and aircraft are available to the majority. The nations have formed an Inter-Continental League of governments so that it is unlikely that war will ever touch us again. And this is merely a beginning. In ten years, continuing our freely competitive way of developing, all will be living on a scale that only the wealthy can afford today."

He came to an end and stared at the Texcocans.

Taller said, "There seems to be no agreement between the two delegations."

Across from him the ancient Honorable Russ said, "It is difficult to measure this progress which both planets advocate. We seem to count refrigerators, television and privately owned cars and houses. You seem to ignore personal standards and concentrate on steel tonnage and the size of the grain harvest."

The Texcocan scientist, Wiss, said easily, "Given the steel mills, and eventually automobiles and refrigerators will run off our assembly lines like water and will be available for everyone, not just for those who can afford to buy them. That is our goal, an abundance for all, and eventually we will reach it."

"Hmmm, eventually," Peter MacDonald laughed nastily.

The atmosphere was suddenly hostile. Hostile beyond anything that had gone before in earlier conference. There was an absolute burden of hate in the air.

And then Martin Gunther said without inflection, "I note that you have removed from the *Pedagogue*'s library all information dealing with nuclear fission."

"For the purpose of study," Dick Hawkins said smoothly.

"Of course," Gunther said. "Did you plan to return it in the immediate future?"

"I am afraid our studies will take some time," Barry Watson said flatly.

"I was afraid so," Gunther said. "Happily, I took the precaution of making microfilms of the material involved more than a year ago."

Barry Watson pushed his chair back and came to his feet. "We seem to have accomplished what little was possible by the meeting," he said. Then, "If anything." He looked to his right and his left at his cohorts. "Let's go, gentlemen."

They came stiffly erect. Watson turned on his heel and started for the door.

As they left, Natt Roberts turned for a moment and said to Gunther, "One thing, Martin. During this next ten years you might consider whether or not half a century has been enough to accomplish our task. Should we consider staying on? I would think the Co-ordinator would accept any recommendation along this line that we might make."

The Genoese delegation looked after him thoughtfully, long after he had gone.

Finally, Martin Gunther said, "Baron Leonar, I think it might be a good idea if you put some of your men to work on making steel alloys suitable for spacecraft. The way things are developing, perhaps we'll need them in the not too distant future."

Buchwald and MacDonald looked at him unblinkingly.

* * * *

It was fifty years to a day since the *Pedagogue* had first gone into orbit about Rigel. Five decades had passed. Half a century.

Of the original crew of the *Pedagogue*, seven now gathered in the lounge of the spaceship. All of them had changed physically. Some of them softer to the point of flabbiness; some harder both of body and soul.

The one representative of the weaker sex had developed a sullen expression as well as an exaggerated sexual one.

Barry Watson, Natt Roberts, Dick Hawkins, Isobel Sanchez, of the Texcocan team.

Martin Gunther, Peter MacDonald, Fredric Buchwald of the Genoese.

The gathering wasn't so large as the one before. Only Taller and the scientist Wiss attended from Texcoco; only Baron Leonar and the son of Honorable Russ, from Genoa.

From the beginning they stared with hostility across the conference table. Even the pretense of amiability was gone.

Barry Watson rapped finally. "I am not going to dwell upon the measures you have been taking that can only be construed as military ones aimed eventually at the Texcocan State."

Martin Gunther laughed nastily. "Is your implication that your own people have not taken the same measures, in fact, inaugurated them?"

Watson said, "As I say, I have no intention of even discussing this. Surely we can arrive at no agreement. There is one point, however, that we should consider on this occasion."

The corpulent Peter MacDonald wheezed. "Well, out with it, then!"

Natt Roberts said, "I mentioned the matter to you at the last meeting."

"Ah, yes," Gunther nodded thoughtfully. "Just as you left. We have considered it. In fact, we held a small meeting just before coming up here."

The Texcocans waited for him to go on.

"If I understand you," Gunther said slowly, "you think we should reconsider returning to Terra City at this time."

"It should be discussed," Watson nodded. "Whatever the, ah, temporary difficulties between us, the original project of the *Pedagogue* is still our duty. Nothing is of more importance to all of us."

The three of the Genoese team nodded their solemn agreement. "Of course," Buchwald murmured.

"And the problem becomes: Have we accomplished completely what we set out to do? And, further, is it necessary, or at least preferable, for us to stay on and continue administration of the progress of the Rigel planets?"

They thought on it.

Buchwald said hesitantly, "It has been my own belief that Genoa is not quite ready for us to let loose the, ah, reins. If we left now, I am not sure..."

Roberts said, "The same applies to Texcoco. The State has made fabulous strides, but I am not sure what would happen if we leaders were to leave. There might be a complete collapse."

Isobel Sanchez muttered, "Oh, I couldn't bear the idea of returning to Terra City. Such a bore, really, life on Terra. So... so uninteresting. So much routine work and so little..."

Dick Hawkins looked at her testily. "That's not at all the point. The point is are we, or are we not *needed* by the people of these planets?"

Barry Watson said, "We seem to be in basic agreement. Is a suggestion in order that we extend, for another twenty-five years, at least, this expedition's work?"

Dick Hawkins said, "The Office of Galactic Colonization..."

Peter MacDonald broke in on him smoothly. "Will undoubtedly send out a ship to investigate. Very well, we shall simply inform them that things are not as yet propitious to our leaving, that another twenty-five years is in order. Since we are on the scene, undoubtedly our recommendation will be heeded."

Watson looked from one Earthling to the next. "Then are we in agreement?"

Each in turn nodded.

Peter MacDonald said, "And do you all realize that here we have a unique situation that might be exploited for the benefit of the whole human race?"

They looked at him, intrigued, but questioningly.

"The dynamic we find in Genoa, and Texcoco, too, for that matter, though we disagree on so many fundamentals, is beyond that in the Solar System. These are new planets, new ambitions are alive. We have at our fingertips, man's highest developments, evolved on Earth. But with this new dynamic, this freshness, might we not in time push even beyond old Earth?"

"You mean..." Natt Roberts said.

MacDonald nodded and pursed fat lips. "What particular value is gained by our uniting Genoa and Texcoco with the so-called Galactic Commonwealth? Why not press ahead on our own? With the vigor of these new races, we might well leave Earth far behind."

Barry Watson mused, "Carrying your suggestion to the ultimate, who is to say that one day Rigel might not become the new center of the human race, rather than Sol?"

"A point well taken," Gunther agreed.

All the others of Earth nodded their solemn agreement.

"No," Taller said softly.

The seven Earthlings turned hostile eyes to him.

"This particular matter does not concern you, General," Watson rapped at him.

The grim visaged Taller smiled his dour amusement at that and came to his feet, to tower above them.

"No," he said. "I am afraid that hard though it might be for you to give up the powers you have held so long, you Earthlings are going to have to return to Terra City, from whence you came."

Isobel said languidly, "Oh, Taller, don't be a flat."

Baron Leonar, however, said in gentle agreement with the general, "But obviously, he is correct."

"What is this?" Watson rapped. "I'm not at all amused."

The Honorable Russ stood also and took his position next to Taller. "There is no longer use of prolonging this. I have heard you Earthlings say, more than once, that man adapts to preserve himself. Very well, we of Genoa and Texcoco are adapting to the present situation. We are of the belief that if you are allowed to remain in power we of the Rigel planets will be destroyed, probably in an atomic holocaust. In self-protection we have found it necessary to unite, we Genoese and Texcocans. We bear you no ill will, far to the contrary, you have brought wonders to us. However, it is necessary that you all return to Earth. You have impressed upon us the aforementioned truism that man adapts but in the *Pedagogue*'s library I have found another that also applies. Power corrupts, and absolute power corrupts absolutely."

There were heavy automatics in the hands of Natt Roberts and Dick Hawkins. Barry Watson leaned back in his chair, his eyes narrow. "How'd you ever expect to get away with this sort of treason, Taller?"

Martin Gunther blurted, "Or you, Russ?"

Wiss, the Texcocan scientist, quiet all this time, held his wrist radio to his mouth and said, "Come in now."

Dick Hawkins thumbed back the hammer of his hand gun.

"Hold it a minute, Dick," Barry Watson rapped. "I don't like this." To Taller he rasped, "What goes on here? Talk up, you're just about a dead man."

And it was then that they heard the scraping on the outer hull.

The Earthlings looked up at the overhead, dumbfounded.

Isobel blurted, "But... but we have the only two spacecraft available. What can that be?"

"I suggest you put up your weapons," Taller said quietly. "At this late stage, I would hate to see further bloodshed. There has been too much already."

In moments, they heard the opening and closing of locks and footsteps along the corridor. The door opened and in came: Leonid Plekhanov, Joe Chessman, Amschel Mayer, Natalie Wieliczka, Mike Dean, Louis Rosetti, an emaciated Jerry Kennedy and Nick Rykov. Their expressions ran from sheepishness to blank haughtiness.

MacDonald bug-eyed. "Dean, Rosetti, Natalie. The Temple monks burned you at the stake!"

They grinned at him, shamefaced. "Guess not," Mike Dean said. "We were kidnapped. They figured we were getting too stute for our own good. We've been teaching basic science, in some phoney monastery."

Watson's face was white. "Joe," he said.

"Yeah," Joe Chessman growled. "You sold me out. But Taller and the Texcocans thought I was still of some use." He looked at Leonid Plekhanov, strangely subdued compared to the man he had been half a century before. "I suppose they did the same to you. Took you off and held you, utilizing your learning."

Amschel Mayer snapped bitterly, "And now if you fools will put down your stupid guns, we'll make the final arrangements for returning this expedition to Terra City. Personally, I'll be glad to get away!"

Behind the resurrected Earthlings were a sea of faces representing the foremost figures of both Texcoco and Genoa in every field of endeavor. At least fifty of them in all.

As though protectively, the Earthlings ganged together at the far side of the mess table they had met over so often.

Martin Gunther, his expression still dazed, said, "I... I don't know. This is impossible. You are all alive!"

Leonid Plekhanov looked about him. "Not quite all," he said lowly. "Cogswell, Stevens, MacBride. We've had a heavy toll."

Taller resumed his spokesmanship. "From the first, the most progressive elements on both Texcoco and Genoa realized the value of your expedition and have been in fundamental sympathy with the aims of the *Pedagogue*, or, at least, its original aims. Primitive life is not idyllic. Until man is free from nature's tyranny and has solved the basic problems of sufficient food, clothing, shelter, medical care and education for all, he is unable to realize himself. So we cooperated with you to the extent we found possible."

His smile was grim. "I am afraid that almost from the beginning, and on both planets, your very actions developed an underground, I believe you call it. Not an overt one, since we needed your assistance to build the new industrialized culture you showed us was possible. We even protected you against yourselves, since it soon became obvious that if left alone you would destroy each other in your mad desire for power."

Baron Leonar broke in. "Don't misunderstand. It wasn't until the past couple of decades that this underground which had sprung up on both planets, united."

Barry Watson blurted, "But Joe... Chessman..." He refused to meet the eyes of the man he had condemned.

Taller said, "From the first you made no effort to study our customs. If you had, you'd have realized why my father allied himself to you after you had killed Taller First. And why I did not take my revenge on Chessman after he had killed Reif. A Khan's first training is that no personal emotion must interfere with the needs of the People. When you turned Joe Chessman over to me, as Leonid Plekhanov earlier was turned over to Reif, I realized his education, his abilities, were too great to destroy. We sent him to a mountain university and have used him profitably all these years. In fact, it was Chessman who finally brought us to space travel."

"That's right," Buchwald blurted. "You've got a spacecraft out there. How could you possibly?"

Taller said mildly, "There are but a handful of you; you could hardly keep track of two whole planets and all that went on upon them."

Amschel Mayer said bitingly, "All this can be gone over on our return to Terra City. We'll have a full year in space to explain to ourselves and each other why we became such complete idiots. I was originally head of this expedition—before my supposed friends railroaded me to prison— does anyone object if I take over again, with Leonid Plekhanov as my deputy?"

"No," Joe Chessman growled.

The others shook their heads.

Taller said, "There is but one other thing. In spite of how you may feel at this moment, basically you have succeeded in your task. That is, you have brought Texcoco and Genoa to an industrialized culture. We hold various reservations about how you accomplished this. However, when you return to your Co-ordinator of Galactic Colonization, please inform him that we are anxious to receive his ambassadors. The term is *ambassadors* and we will expect to meet on a basis of equality. Surely in all Earth's social evolution, man has worked out something better than either of your teams have built here. We should like to be instructed."

Dick Hawkins said stiffly, "We can instruct you on Earth's present socioeconomic system."

"I am afraid we no longer trust you, Richard Hawkins. Send others, uncorrupted by power, privilege or great wealth."

* * * *

When they had gone and the sound of their departing spacecraft had faded, Amschel Mayer snapped, "We might as well get underway. And cheer up, confound it, we have lots of time to contrive a reasonable report for the Co-ordinator."

Jerry Kennedy managed a thin grin, almost reminiscent of the younger Kennedy of the first years on Genoa. "Say," he said, "I wonder if well be granted a good long vacation before being sent on another assignment."

* * * *

They met in the library, behind the racks of tapes and she looked up into his face, warily.

He said, his voice husky, "Hi, Polack."

She reached up and traced a finger along a scar that ran from temple to chin.

He said, "An assassin got through my guards one day." He reached for her, but she moved back, shaking her head.

"I... I don't know..." she said. "You're not the same."

He looked at her bitterly. "Are you?"

"No. No, I suppose not. We're both different. We'll have to start all over. Learn to know each other, all over. Too many things have happened, Barry."

He let his hands drop to his sides.

"All right," he said. "As Amschel said, we have a full year." He grinned suddenly, wryly. "We'll have to start changing my character right away if I'm going to be acceptable again in that short a time."

ABOUT THE AUTHOR

Dallas McCord ('Mack') Reynolds was born in California in 1917. His father was the Socialist Labor Party Presidential Candidate on two occasions, and Reynolds' life and work were deeply affected by his political upbringing. After early careers in newspapers and computing, Reynolds returned from the Second World War and began to write science fiction. Based in Mexico but travelling widely in his role as Travel Editor for a men's magazine, he started slowly but surely to sell his work. Mack Reynolds wrote the first *Star Trek* novel, *Mission to Horatius*, and was once voted Most popular SF Author by the readers of *Galaxy Science Fiction* magazine. He died in 1983.

Contents

www.ingramcontent.com/pod-product-compliance
Lightning Source LLC
Chambersburg PA
CBHW022039170626
46808CB00003B/1280